Pra

Vulnerable

Here's what some readers have to say about the first book in the McIntyre Security Bodyguard Series...

"I can't even begin to explain how much I loved this book! The plot, your writing style, the dialogue and OMG those vivid descriptions of the characters and the setting were so AMAZING!"
– Dominique

"I just couldn't put it down. The first few pages took my breath away. I realized I had stumbled upon someone truly gifted at writing." – Amanda

"*Vulnerable* is an entertaining, readable erotic romance with a touch of thriller adding to the tension. Fans of the *Fifty Shades* series will enjoy the story of wildly rich and amazingly sexy Shane and his newfound love, the young, innocent Beth, who needs his protection." – Sheila

"I freaking love it! I NEED book 2 now!!!" – Laura

"Shane is my kind of hero. I loved this book. I am anxiously waiting for the next books in this series." – Tracy

Praise for
Fearless

Here's what some readers have to say about the
second book in the McIntyre Security Bodyguard Series...

"Fearless is officially my favourite book of the year. I adore April
Wilson's writing and this book is the perfect continuation to the
McIntyre Security Bodyguard Series."
– Alice Laybourne, Lunalandbooks

"I highly recommend for a read that will provide nail biting
suspense along with window fogging steam and
sigh worthy romance."
– Catherine Bibby of Rochelle's Reviews

Books by April Wilson

McIntyre Security Bodyguard Series:

Vulnerable

Fearless

Shane (book 2.5 novella)

Broken

Shattered

Imperfect

Ruined

Hostage

Redeemed

Marry Me (novella)

Snowbound (novella)

Regret (coming 2019)

plus lots more coming...

snowbound

McIntyre Security Inc.
Bodyguard Series
Book 10
(a novella)

april wilson

Wilson Publishing
P.O. Box 292913
Dayton, OH 45429
www.aprilwilsonauthor.com

Visit www.aprilwilsonauthor.com to sign up for the author's e-mail newsletter to be notified about upcoming releases.

ISBN: 9781797442600

Published in the United States of America
First Printing February 2019

Dedications

For Shane and Beth.
Thank you for inhabiting my imagination.

Acknowledgements

I was captivated by the idea of Beth and Luke being stranded in Clancy's during a freak blizzard that would temporarily cripple downtown Chicago. In the story, Sam tells about how his mother remembers the Blizzard of '78 in Dayton, Ohio, where she and her son grew up. I remember that blizzard well! I was one of those school-aged kids trying to walk home through waist-deep snow.

As always, I owe a huge debt of gratitude to my sister, Lori, for being there with me every step of the way. Her tireless support and encouragement are priceless.

Thank you to Sue Vaughn Boudreaux for her unwavering support. Sue is an invaluable help to me and instrumental at keeping me on track.

Thanks to Becky Morean and Julie Collier for being such good friends!

Finally, I want to thank all of my readers around the world and the members of my reader group on Facebook. I am so incredibly blessed to have you in my life. Your love and support and enthusiasm are invaluable. You've become dear friends to me, and I am grateful for you all. Thank you from the very bottom of my heart for every review, like, share, and comment. I wouldn't be able to do the thing that I love to do most—share my characters and their stories—without your amazing support. Every day, I wake up and thank my lucky stars!

With much love to you all... April

1

Beth McIntyre

I t's snowing," Sam says as he walks through the open door to my office carrying two bright red holiday cups with lids. "It looks like we'll have a white Christmas after all."

The holiday music coming through the store's sound system reminds me that tomorrow is Christmas. It will be Luke's first Christmas! I can't believe my baby is six months old. It seems like just yesterday he entered this world under a cloud of trauma and fear. It hasn't always been smooth sailing, and I've had more than my fair share of challenges adjusting to motherhood. But thankfully, in large part because of Shane's unwavering patience and support, I've made the adjustment. I already have my Christmas presents—my husband and my son. They're all I need.

My bodyguard hands me one of the steaming cups. "I come bearing gifts."

The warm cup feels good in my hands. I sniff the steam coming out of the sipping spout. "Mmm, chocolate."

"Not just any chocolate," he clarifies. "Peppermint hot chocolate with whipped cream and chocolate sprinkles. Your favorite."

"I love you," I say, sighing as I take a tentative sip of the hot, creamy mixture. *Ah, sweet chocolatey goodness. Just what I need.*

"I know you do." Sam heads to the sofa where he likes to kick back and relax while we're at the store, propping his boots up on the coffee table while I work at my desk. He stops in front of the large picture window that overlooks North Michigan Avenue and the bustling shopping district of downtown Chicago known as *The Magnificent Mile*. "It's really coming down now."

I hop up from my desk chair and join him at the window. He's not kidding. The white stuff's really coming down in big fat flakes. I'd heard the forecast was for a few inches of snow today, but this looks like much more than that. "We're definitely going to have a white Christmas."

A side door to my office opens, and Lindsey Carmichael's smiling face appears. Big brown eyes dominate a pretty face framed by a cloud of curly brown hair. "Guess who's awake and hungry?"

Lindsey is a godsend. She was working the sales floor as a part-time employee—one of the many college students who work here—when I first started bringing Luke to work with me. She'd find any excuse to come up to my office to fawn over him. She's a real baby magnet, and Luke took to her right away.

As the eldest of ten kids, Lindsey has tons of childcare experience—just what I needed. So, I offered her a promotion, and she's now Luke's nanny here at Clancy's Bookshop on the days when I'm here.

I set my hot chocolate on my desk and meet Lindsey halfway.

Looking like he just woke up, Luke squints his soft blue eyes as he adjusts to the lights. When he sees me, he grins, revealing the tip of his first little tooth peeking out of his bottom gum. He reaches for me. "Mum-mum-mum-mum-mum."

Luke has become increasingly vocal in just the past couple of weeks. His first utterance was "mum-mum-mum." Poor Shane has been trying to get him to say *da-da*, but he hasn't had any luck so far.

"There's my sweet boy," I say, grinning at my son as I take him from Lindsey. I prop him on my hip and kiss his forehead. He grasps my sweater in one tight little fist, and he presses his free hand to his mouth and starts sucking loudly.

Sam chuckles as he gently brushes his hand over Luke's tufts of blond hair. "Definitely hungry."

"I changed his diaper and his clothes," Lindsey says, smiling brightly. The twenty-year-old is practically bouncing on her feet.

Luke looks very handsome in his black knit sweatpants, a gray-and-white striped hoodie shirt, and white socks. He squirms in my arms, squawking softly as he turns his face toward me and nuzzles my blouse. Yes, he's hungry.

Lindsey sniffs the air. "Do I smell chocolate?"

"Peppermint hot chocolate," I say. "Why don't you run downstairs to the café and have some while I nurse Luke."

"You don't have to tell me twice," she says, heading for the door with an excited wave.

"Don't forget the whipped cream and sprinkles!" Sam calls after her.

Before heading into the attached nursery, I glance out the window, amazed at how hard the snow is coming down now. The air is so thick with snow I can barely make out the tall buildings across the street. "Have you seen the updated forecast?" I ask Sam. "How much snow are they predicting?"

He shakes his head as he pulls out his phone. "I'll check."

Luke lets out a plaintive cry as he throws his head against my shoulder and sticks his thumb in his mouth. "Mum-mum-mum," he says around his thumb.

"Okay, sweetie, we're going. Poor baby." And then to Sam, I say, "Be back soon."

I carry Luke into his nursery, closing the door behind us. This space used to be a rather sizable storage room, but Shane had it remodeled for Luke. Now the walls are painted a soft gray with white trim. There are dimmable lights recessed along the edges of the ceiling, with a few additional light fixtures suspended overhead. A small bathroom was added for convenience.

I settle into the upholstered glider, holding Luke on my lap while I use my other hand to unbutton my blouse. As soon as I unclip the nursing cup over my right breast, he starts squirming and reaching for me. "Hang on, peanut. It's coming."

I'm amazed at how far we've come since the early days, when I struggled so much with nursing. Luke had trouble latching on, but I think that was mostly the result of my own issues with postpartum depression. As someone who struggles constantly with anxiety, I really took a tailspin after Luke's traumatic and premature birth.

I lay the nursing pillow across my lap and position Luke on his side, facing me. He latches on eagerly, and I rock us gently as he nurses. He gazes up at me, his blue eyes locked steadfastly onto mine. I brush my hand over his pale-blond hair and wonder if he'll grow up to be blond, like me, or if his hair will darken later to Shane's chocolate brown shade.

I stroke his forehead lightly with the tip of my finger, mesmerized by how soft his skin is. He reaches out and latches onto my finger, holding it tightly in his little fist. I watch his chest rise and fall with each breath and listen to the muffled chuffing sounds he makes as he suckles.

Memories of his birth come flooding back, sudden and painful. I swear I can smell the hot, musty air of the attic space where Shane's youngest sister, Lia—acting as my bodyguard—hid me during the robbery of the convenience store below us. My heart starts hammering in my chest, which feels like it's being squeezed in a vice. My thoughts are racing, and I have to fight to rein them in. A heavy weight presses down on me, hampering my breathing. Taking a deep breath, I lean my head back and close my eyes. *Calm down. Everything's fine. Luke's fine. You're fine. There's nothing to be afraid of. Just relax and enjoy this moment.*

I take several slow, measured breaths, breathing in through my nose and out through my mouth. I've been practicing meditation and yoga to help me cope with anxiety, and it's been helping.

I repeat my mantra over and over, hoping I can convince myself that it's true. Calm down. *Everything's fine....*

I can make out the quiet strains of Christmas melodies being piped throughout the store's sound system. It's loud enough that I can make out the tune, but not loud enough to disturb Luke when he's sleeping. Right now, Bing Crosby is dreaming of a white Christmas, and I smile because it looks like we're going to have one this year.

Shane wanted me to stay home today, being that it was Christmas Eve, and there would be a crazy number of shoppers downtown on what is one of the busiest shopping days of the holiday season. But I didn't want to miss the festivities. Erin has all kinds of activities planned today... giveaways, door prizes, contests for the kids, free Christmas cookies and hot chocolate, even a Santa Claus. I didn't want to miss out on all of that.

My phone chimes with an incoming text message, and I manage to pull my phone out of my pocket without disturbing Luke.

It's snowing, sweetheart. Are you planning to head home soon?

Shane's message makes me smile.

Yes, I noticed the snow. It's lovely. We'll have a white Christmas after all.

A moment later, he texts again:

Where's Joe?

Joe, my driver. I reply:

I sent him home this morning as we won't need him until later this afternoon.

My phone is silent for a few moments, and I can just picture Shane weighing his next words. My husband is very protective, some would say overprotective. He tries hard, though, not to smother me. Sometimes it's a tough line for him to straddle.

Another text comes in:

Sam is there?

I smile as I reply:

Yes. He's in my office.

I have to chuckle at his question. Of course Sam's here. He's my full-time bodyguard. Sam goes wherever Luke and I go, and nothing short of a hurricane could separate him from me. Shane knows that full well.

I text him again:

We're fine. Please don't worry.

He's silent for a while, and I imagine him working through his options. Then he sends me this:

I'm a husband and a father, sweetheart. It's my job to worry. I'll call Joe and ask him to wait there on-site with the Escalade. Please be home before dark.

At this time of year, it's dark by four-thirty, but that's hours away still.

Smiling at Shane's reply—his idea of a compromise, I'm sure—I lift Luke to my shoulder and pat his back. He's clearly not pleased by the interruption of his meal, but I keep at it until he finally burps.

Once he has cooperated, I transfer him to my other breast and he resumes nursing.

As his perfect, little rosebud of a mouth works at my nipple, I think back to the time we spent living in the neonatal intensive care unit at Children's Hospital. I struggled to nurse him. I struggled to bond with him. I would use any excuse to get someone else to take care of my baby, someone other than myself. His father, his nurse, his aunts and uncles and grandparents. Anyone other than me.

Post-partum depression is a frightening thing. I was riddled with anxiety and drowning in my fear that I would be a horrible mother. I was terrified that I'd be incapable of caring for a fragile, newborn infant.

As Luke lays his tiny palm on my breast, I trace his pale blond eyebrows with the tip of my index finger. "Thank you for being patient with me." My throat tightens, and I know tears aren't far away. "I love you, my little peanut."

Once Luke is satisfied, his belly full, I check his diaper—still dry—and carry him into my office. Sam's pacing the floor, his phone to his ear. "I know!" he says, brushing his hand over his beard. When he catches sight of me, he comes to a stop. "She's here. I'll talk to you later." After a pause, he says, "I love you too." And then he ends the call and pockets his phone.

I smile. "Was that Cooper?" *Cooper, my adopted father. Sam's boyfriend.*

"Yeah. He and Shane are worried about this weather. The forecast is now calling for six to eight inches of accumulation by nightfall, and the temperature is dropping fast. He and Shane both want you and Luke to go home."

I glance out the window and see nothing but billowing clouds of white. It really is turning into a winter wonderland. Just the thought of going outside in that cold, blustery storm makes me shiver. "Let's go downstairs and grab some lunch in the café. Then we'll think about heading home."

Sam opens the door for me. "By the way, in case you don't already know, your husband wants you home, like yesterday."

As I walk past him, Sam holds his hands out to Luke. "Come here, peanut," he says.

Fearlessly, Luke throws himself at Sam, who catches him in his very capable hands.

When we reach the bottom of the curving staircase, Sam follows me to the double glass doors, and together we survey the sidewalk and street outside. At eye level, I can see that the snow is accumulating rather quickly—far more so than I realized. And the wind is wreaking havoc with the snow, blowing it into tall drifts along the edges of the street, some as high as the trashcans and newspaper stands.

Mack has several of our maintenance guys outside clearing off the sidewalk in front of the store and putting down salt, but it seems like the snow is falling faster than they can clear it away. Beyond the sidewalks, the snow is rapidly piling up in the street, causing traffic to slow to a crawl.

I peer outside our doors, looking up and down the street as far as I can see. In the distance, I hear sirens blaring. This doesn't feel good. My chest tightens with the realization that it's going to be difficult getting home. I'm not worried for myself, but rather for my son, who's currently patting Sam's bearded cheek and mumbling *mum-mum*. I meet Sam's gaze. "Shane asked Joe to come get us."

Sam nods, his expression perfectly relaxed. If he's at all concerned, he doesn't show it. "Good." He doesn't bother to say what we're both thinking. *The sooner we get Luke home, the better.*

He reaches for his phone with his free hand to check a weather app. "Looks like it's going to snow all afternoon and evening." He shows me the weather forecast, which shows nothing in our immediate future but snow and more snow.

Mack joins us at the doors, standing on my other side. "The snow's really coming down hard, Beth. And it's icy. I think you should head out. Where's Joe?"

"Shane called him. We'll go when he arrives."

A car loses traction in front of the store and skids into the oncoming traffic. The driver slams on his horn, but that does nothing to stop the forward momentum. The driver is unable to regain control, and the car skids across the center line and hits another car head-on. I cringe at the sound of metal crunching on metal. Thankfully, none of the cars are moving fast right now. Both of the drivers get out of their cars, unscathed, but upset as they face off in the street.

Because of the minor wreck out front, traffic has practically crawled to a halt, and angry drivers are laying on their horns.

Mack pulls out his phone. "I'll call it in."

On my other side, Sam says, "Yeah, we need to get you guys home."

Luke pivots toward me, leaning away from Sam as he reaches for me. "Mum-mum-mum."

I take him from Sam, and Luke reaches for one of my earrings.

"Oh, no you don't," I tell him, intercepting his little fingers.

As Mack ends the call to 911, his phone chimes with an incoming notification. As he reads the notice, his expression tightens. "Chicago has declared a Level One Snow Emergency. *Roadways are hazardous due to blowing and drifting snow,*" he says, quoting the message, chuckling. "No kidding." He slips his phone into his pocket. "Definitely time for you to leave. In fact, you might want to think about closing the store early. I know it's a big shopping day, but with the way traffic is going, I think we should let the employees head home soon."

I nod. "I'll make an announcement."

"Beth?"

Hearing my name, I glance toward the check-out counter. Erin's waving at me to come over.

"Excuse me," I say. Sam follows me to the check-out.

When I join Erin behind the counter, she pulls me aside, gesturing at one of the employees standing at a register. The young woman, Kayla, very obviously pregnant, is just a couple weeks from her due date.

"Kayla should go home," Erin whispers. "She shouldn't be out in this snowstorm. In fact, we should send everyone home."

I nod. "Mack and I were just talking about that."

Customers are starting to gather at the doors and store windows, watching the snow fall, talking in hushed voices as they furiously send text messages. The longer people stay out in this weather, the harder it's going to be for them to get home. "Let's close the store," I say.

Erin's blue eyes widen, and she tucks her chin-length dark hair behind her ear. "I'll make an announcement."

"Tell them the store is closing at noon. That will give everyone twenty minutes to finish up what they need to do and check out."

Erin gets on the speaker system and makes the announcement, alerting both customers and staff. The customers who are still in the store start heading toward the checkout lanes in droves. Erin taps Kayla on the shoulder. "You should go now," she tells the pregnant woman. "I'll have someone cover for you."

Looking more than a little pale, Kayla nods gratefully to Erin as she heads for the employee's locker room to collect her things.

While we're waiting for Joe to arrive—undoubtedly the snow has slowed him down—Sam and I head for the café to grab a quick bite to eat while we still can. Luke's fidgeting, and I think he's still hungry. Sam runs up to my office to grab my diaper bag, and he brings it down to the café. Erin joins us, and the three of us sit at a table by the windows so we can monitor the developments outside.

"Do you want some cereal?" I ask Luke, balancing him carefully on my lap while I retrieve the supplies needed to mix up his infant cereal. As soon as he sees me pull out his bowl and a plastic baby spoon, he starts bouncing on my lap, cooing loudly and slapping his hands on the table.

Sam scoops Luke off my lap and onto his. "Come here, peanut, before you fall off your mommy's lap."

From where we're sitting near the front windows, we can easily see that the sidewalks are becoming increasingly empty as fewer and fewer pedestrians brave the weather. The few that are out on the sidewalks look like they're struggling against the blowing snow. The street on the other hand, is packed bumper to bumper with cars, buses, and taxis that don't look like they're going anywhere anytime soon. I hear more sirens off in the distance, their shrill alarms sending chills down my spine.

As I finish mixing Luke's cereal, I watch him with a growing sense of unease. I wish we'd stayed home today, as Shane had wanted. Then we wouldn't be out in this storm. Luke would be at home, safe and sound, where he should be. Maybe I am a terrible mother after all.

As I fasten a bib around Luke's neck, my phone chimes with an incoming message. Sam takes the baby spoon from me and proceeds to feed my son while I read the text. I hope it's Joe, telling us he's here. But no. It's from Shane. My pulse kicks up, because I know he's worried about us. He's too kind to tell me *I told you so*, but he doesn't have to say it. I already know.

I hope you'll be heading home soon.

I can easily read between the lines and hear the tension in his message. I reply:

As soon as Joe arrives, we'll go. I promise.

My unease grows. The situation outside is deteriorating quickly, going from bad to worse with each passing moment. Our window of opportunity for getting home safely is rapidly closing.

2

Beth McIntyre

I think this storm qualifies as a blizzard," Sam says, sipping hot chocolate as we watch out the window.

It looks like a complete white-out, with visibility almost nil thanks to the blowing snow.

Just as he says that, a car out in front of the store slides on the ice, losing control as it turns ninety degrees and slams sideways into a light pole. The car directly behind it, unable to stop in time, rear ends the first car. Then a horrible chain reaction occurs, and suddenly four cars are involved. The public bus behind them manages to stop in time, but that side of the street is completely blocked now, preventing cars from driving past.

My heart is now hammering in my chest, and I look at Sam. I'm sure I look as panicked as I feel. I'm terrible when it comes to hiding my emotions—it's why I never play poker with Shane and his siblings. Joe's not going to be able to get the Escalade anywhere near the bookstore.

Sam lays his hand on my shoulder and squeezes gently. "It's all right. We'll get you and Luke home as soon as possible."

A feeling of dread comes over me, and my vision starts to darken along the edges as if I'm staring down a long, narrow tunnel. I feel a crushing weight on my chest, squeezing my ribs and lungs, making breathing difficult.

Sam watches me closely. "Do you need something?"

I know he's referring to my rescue inhaler, which is upstairs in my purse. I left it in my desk drawer. I shake my head, trying to rein in my anxiety before I do end up having an asthma attack. I take a slow, deep breath. "I'm okay."

Sam hands me Luke's spoon. "Here, you feed him. It will give you something to do."

I nod, swallowing hard. Feeding Luke isn't going to change anything about our situation, but I feel like I should be doing something for him. Holding him, protecting him, is all I can do right now. I would give anything to wave a magic wand and teleport us all to the safety of our penthouse apartment, but that's not going to happen.

Mack walks up to our table and drops down into the only empty chair. "It's a Level Two Snow Emergency now," he says in a low voice. "It looks like all of the customers have left, and the employees are leaving now. Security is doing a sweep of the building to make sure everyone is gone."

Employees, bundled up in winter coats, hats, and scarves, stream out the front doors, heading to their preferred modes of transportation, mostly buses and the L. The L train should be able to run all right, as it's elevated above the street—and therefore free of the congested street traffic—but the public buses... I doubt they're doing well. My hope is that the side streets are faring better.

My phone chimes with a text message from Joe.

I'm parked in the garage. That's as close as I could get. I'll come to you. Sit tight.

Relief sweeps through me. The parking garage is just two blocks away, but with help from both Joe and Sam, we'll manage just fine. I've already decided that Erin should come back to the penthouse with us. I don't want her trying to catch a bus to Rogers Park, where she shares an apartment with three college friends.

I reply to Joe:

Thank you. Be careful.

Then my phone rings, and I jump. It's Shane! "Shane! Hi."

"Hi, sweetheart." He sounds perfectly calm, but I have a feeling he's putting on an act for my sake. I'm sure he knows I'm worried. "How's it going? Is Joe there yet?"

"I'm fine. And yes, Joe just called from the parking garage—he couldn't get any closer. He's on his way here now, and then we'll all walk to the Escalade."

Shane blows out a heavy breath. "As soon as he arrives, I want you heading for the vehicle, okay?"

"We will. Are you heading home, too?"

"As soon as I know you're safely home, I'll leave. Let me talk to Sam."

I hand my phone to Sam. "Shane wants to talk to you."

Erin walks up behind me, laying her hand on my shoulder. She looks a bit frantic. "We have a serious problem," she whispers in a shaky voice. "It's Kayla."

"What about her?"

"She's in the bathroom, crying. Her water broke. She hasn't been able to reach her husband, and when she called 911 for transport to the hospital, they told her they're not sure how soon they can get here. There are accidents all over the city apparently, and the emergency services are slammed. Traveling anywhere downtown right now is difficult."

I can feel the blood drain from my face, leaving my cheeks ice cold. With a flash, I remember the exact moment my water broke. Lia and I were hiding in the attic room over a convenient store with gun fire below us. What a nightmare—then and now. Kayla must be scared to death. "Okay, let me think."

"Beth!" Joe Rucker is heading right for me, his face flushed from both exertion and the freezing temperature. He's dressed in a winter parka, with a gray wool scarf wrapped around his neck and a black knit hat covering his head. "It's bad out there," he says, breathless as he pulls his hat off, revealing closely trimmed white hair that contrasts starkly with his mocha complexion. "North Michigan is a parking lot—no vehicles can get through. But we can still make it home if we stick to the side streets."

My stomach sinks, because I know I can't leave Kayla in distress. I know what I have to do. And I know how angry Shane's going to be. "Joe, I need you to do me a favor. It's important."

He frowns, narrowing his dark eyes with a fair dose of skepticism, as if he knows he's not going to like what I say next. "What?"

"I need you to take one of my employees to the hospital. She's—"

"No." He shakes his head, stopping me mid-sentence. His low voice drops even lower. "My orders are clear. I'm to get you and Lucas home safely, ASAP. Sam, too."

My shoulders fall as I know I won't be able to keep my word to Shane. "Joe, I can't leave now. One of my employees is pregnant, and her water just broke. She could be in labor already, and the paramedics don't know when they'll be able to get here. She needs to get to the hospital right now, and you're the only one who can take her."

Hands propped on his hips, Joe scowls and shakes his head vehemently. "Beth, I can't. I'm sorry."

"Joe, please!" I hand Luke to Sam and rise from my chair to stand face-to-face with my driver. He towers over me, a muscular hulk of a man, a gentle giant who looks every bit like the former heavyweight boxer he used to be. I stare up into his eyes, hardening my expression and my words. "I'm not leaving this store until she's safely at the hospital."

Joe shakes his head, clearly conflicted. "Shane will have my head if I go against his orders."

"No, he won't. He'll understand. But right now, Kayla's our top priority. We have to help her. I won't go home knowing one of my employees is in trouble."

Mack stands, offering me his silent support as he tries to reason with Joe. "You know she won't leave under these conditions," he says. "You might as well stop arguing with her and do this. The sooner you get Kayla to the hospital, the sooner you can get back here for Beth and the baby."

I hate putting Joe in this position, but it can't be helped. "Luke and I will be perfectly safe here in this building, Joe. Kayla won't. She needs to get to the hospital."

"I won't leave this building until everyone is safely away," Mack tells Joe. "Beth's right—she'll be perfectly safe here. We have plenty of food and water. We have heat and electricity. We'll be fine."

A noise draws our attention, essentially putting an end to our argument. Kayla is shuffling slowly towards us, holding her distended belly in her hands. Her cheeks are streaked with tears, and it's clear from her expression that she's frightened and in pain.

Joe shakes his head, sighing heavily in resignation. He wags his finger at me. "Your husband is going to fire me for insubordination."

I smile in relief. "No, he won't. I guarantee it."

Mack's phone chimes with an alert notification. "It's a Level Three emergency now," he says, meeting my gaze. "All traffic is prohibited now, except for emergency vehicles."

"Well, Joe's vehicle is an emergency vehicle," I say, walking to Kayla's side and putting my arm around her.

The poor girl is shaking like a leaf, and she leans into me for support. "I'm so sorry, Mrs. McIntyre—"

"You have nothing to be sorry for. Now listen to me—my friend Joe is going to take you to the hospital," I tell her. "He'll be your ambulance."

Erin bundles Kayla into her winter gear and wraps a bright red scarf around her neck and face.

"Thank you," Kayla says. And then she tightens her grip on her belly and grimaces with what I suspect is a contraction.

"Come on, young lady," Joe says with a resigned sigh as he puts one arm around her for support. "My vehicle is parked two blocks from here, and the snow is deep. We'd better get a move on."

Joe looks hard at Sam and Mack. "You two had better damn well make sure you take good care of Beth and Luke, or you won't just have Shane to deal with. You'll have me to deal with, too." Then he leads Kayla toward the front doors. Mack goes with them to let them out and relock the doors.

All of the staff are gone now except for us and the rest of the security team. Half of the lights have been turned down to let everyone outside know the store is closed.

After Joe and Kayla depart, Sam and Erin and I sit down at our little café table as reality sinks in. Our ride home is gone. Luke and I can't leave. And it's too late for Erin to leave. The public buses have stopped running. Perhaps even the L train, too.

When her grandmother passed away last year, Erin essentially became an orphan. She has no other close relatives. I'm the closest thing to family she has now, and I feel responsible for her. She's become like a little sister to me.

"You can come home with us," I tell her. "Assuming we can ever leave."

She brightens, giving me a grateful smile. "Thanks."

Luke has long since finished his cereal and a little bottle of water I gave him. Now he's nodding off in Sam's arms, barely able to keep his eyes open. I should take him upstairs to his crib. As I'm gathering up the diaper bag, my phone rings. The sound wakes Luke and he gives a half-hearted cry before Sam settles him on his shoulder and pats his back. I check my phone screen, not surprised to see it's my husband calling. Again. Crap. I'm not looking forward to this conversation.

Taking a deep breath, I paste a smile on my face as I accept the call. "Hi, honey," I say, trying to sound upbeat.

Shane gets right to the point, his voice terse. "Sweetheart, what's going on? Why aren't you on your way home yet?"

How does he know—oh, right. GPS. He's tracking my phone. "Well—"

"Isn't Joe there yet?"

"He was."

"What do you mean was?"

"One of my employees is in labor. Her water broke, and I asked Joe to take her to the hospital."

"Why didn't you call 911 and have them send an ambulance for her?"

"She did call 911, but they said they didn't know when they could get here. And since Joe had the Escalade parked only a couple of blocks away, I knew he'd be able to get her to the hospital faster than anything."

Shane sighs, and I can just picture him running his fingers through his hair. "Sweetheart, that was your ride home."

"I know, and I'm sorry. But, honestly, I didn't have any other choice. Please don't worry. We're perfectly safe where we are until the storm passes. We have everything we need... food, drinks, heat, power. We're fine."

"I'm going to hang up and call Mack."

"All right," I say, and then end the call.

The store seems eerily quiet now, as there's just a handful of us left. Besides Luke and me, there's Sam, Erin, Mack, and two other security guards.

Suddenly, I feel a bit shaky as reality sinks in. We're essentially stranded here for who knows how long.

Sam's phone rings, and he answers. "Hey, Cooper." He listens for a moment as he leans back in his chair, holding a sleeping baby to his broad chest. "Yeah, she's right here. She's fine." Another pause. "Yes, he's fine too. He's sound asleep, completely oblivious to all the excitement." Then Sam looks at me, his expression serious. "I know. I will." Another pause. Then, "No, honestly she's doing fine."

Sam ends the call and glances my way. "Your husband and my boyfriend are worried about you, and they're both pissed as hell that your ride left without you."

I flinch, afraid of that. "I didn't have a choice, Sam. I couldn't leave her to fend for herself."

Sam smiles as he pats Luke's padded bottom. "Don't worry about it, princess. They'll get over it. They're just a couple of old worry warts."

That makes me laugh. "I'm going to tell them you said that."

A moment later, we hear a deafening boom coming from outside the building. Our lights flicker once, twice, then cut out completely, leaving us in near total darkness. My heart slams in my chest.

Erin jumps to her feet with a cry. "Oh, my God! What just happened?"

"It's all right," Sam says in a reassuring voice as he rises to his feet. "Don't panic. The emergency generators—"

A second later, the emergency lights flicker on throughout the store.

"Everyone all right?" Mack says, as he returns to the café to check on us. He glances out the windows, up and down the street. "A transformer must have blown. It looks like the entire block has lost power."

My body starts shaking as I quickly clear off our table. "Let's take Luke upstairs to his crib."

Sam rises, holding Luke against his chest with one arm. He lays his free arm across my shoulders and gives me a side hug. "Don't worry. We'll be perfectly fine."

❧ 3

Beth McIntyre

It's only one o'clock in the afternoon, but it's already looking like dusk outside. The air is choked with snow so dense we can't even see the other side of the street. Thanks to the power outage, the street lights are out, as are the traffic lights, and the early darkness casts an unsettling pall over the wintery landscape.

After changing his diaper and dressing him in a warm sleeper, I lay Luke in his crib. He rubs his eyes, then turns on his side and yawns, letting sleep overtake him.

I join my friends at my office window. From what we can see of it, North Michigan Avenue is littered with abandoned cars, the result of numerous fender benders and immovable gridlock. The cars' oc-cupants simply walked away, probably hoping to find either a taxi or public transportation home. Most of the collisions occurred at slow speeds, thank goodness, and it appears no one was seriously hurt. Only a small handful of people remain outside as they contemplate their next steps, some of them bundled up, but most of them poorly dressed to weather the storm.

It will likely be fully dark in a couple of hours, but we have our emergency lights, and the generator will keep the lights going all night.

"How much battery life do you have left on your phones?" I ask Erin and Sam.

Sam pulls out his phone and checks the screen. "Seventy-eight percent."

Erin looks at hers and frowns. "Twenty-four percent."

"Don't worry," Mack says as he walks into my office. "I have some portable battery chargers. You're welcome to use them. They'll keep your phones operable through the night."

It looks like we'll be stuck here all night. There's no way the city streets will be cleared and passable before morning. Maybe not even then. I'm struck by a sudden and sharp pang of longing for Shane. He's at the McIntyre Security building today, where he has a private apartment attached to his corner office. He'll be perfectly comfort-able weathering out the storm. But I miss him terribly. There's an ache in my chest, and it feels like the physical distance between us is much greater than just a few miles.

I want him here. I know I'm with good friends, and I know Luke and I will be safe here—Mack and Sam will make sure of it. But spending the rest of the day, and most likely the entire night, without Shane? I hate the thought.

We watch out the window as an older man dressed in a heavy winter coat, hat, and gloves walks down the center of the street. The snow is up to his thighs already, and he's struggling to slog through the heavy stuff.

"My mom used to tell me stories about the Blizzard of '78," Sam says. "She was a kid living in Dayton when they were hit with a record-breaking blizzard. She and her siblings and the neighborhood kids were at school when it happened. It took them *hours* to walk home in snow up to their waists. The big kids walked in the front, forging a path for the smaller kids in the rear. They struggled through the snow, in single file, each kid holding on to the one in front of him. She said it was the most exciting thing they'd ever experienced."

"At least we're in here, and not out there," Erin says.

I put my arm across her shoulders and pull her to my side. "We'll be fine. Just think of it as an impromptu sleepover."

I'm trying to sound upbeat for Erin's sake, but inside I don't feel it. I'd give anything to be at home with Shane right now, snuggling on the sofa in front of the fire and watching the snow fall from the safety and comfort of our penthouse apartment.

"You three might as well make yourselves comfortable in here," Mack says, referring to my office. "My guys and I will remain down on the main floor, keeping an eye on things."

"Keeping an eye on *things*?" I say. "What kind of things?"

Mack smiles as he shrugs. "Nothing. We just want to keep busy."

"Looters," Sam says, earning a sharp look of reproof from Mack.

"Looters?" Erin repeats, her voice rising a notch as she looks to Mack for confirmation.

Despite the fact that Mack is openly scowling at him, Sam nods. "Looters are going to take advantage of the storm and attempt to steal whatever they can. And right now, we're sitting on a ton of cash."

My stomach sinks like a stone. "Oh, my God, I never thought of that." Because of the storm, no one was able to make a bank deposit today. That means we've got a lot of cash on hand. "That wouldn't happen here, would it? Not in such a visible location."

Sam shrugs as he glances out at the street. "It doesn't look like such a visible location right now."

Mack glares at Sam. "Stop scaring them."

Sam shrugs. "Hey, the girls need to be aware of the risks. We're safe in here, yes—*from the storm*. But there could be criminal elements out tonight taking advantage of the fact that the power is out and the cops are spread too thin. As we already learned in Kayla's case, calling 911 right now is pointless. The authorities simply can't move around easily in the city right now."

"Relax, ladies," Mack says, looking and sounding perfectly at ease. "My guys and I will be on duty all night, watching the doors and windows. No one is coming into this store. You have my word on it."

"We have some fleece blankets in the gift department," Erin says, perking up. "Those will come in handy if the temperature drops inside the store. And we have some scarves and hats, too. Even small, decorative pillows."

"Right, no electricity," I say, realizing that our loss of power affects more than just the lights. "That means no heat." And no power to the appliances in the café. No more hot water. No coffee. And the perishable items in the refrigerated case might spoil, depending on how long the power stays off.

"We'll be okay," Sam says. "We have our coats and hats. And if we have to, we can all huddle together on the sofa to stay warm."

Erin rushes off to gather up some blankets and pillows and whatever other supplies she thinks might be useful.

Sam heads back down to the café to collect some snacks and hot drinks. "We might as well use up what's left of the hot water while we can," he says. He returns with a cup of hot coffee for himself and two hot chocolates for me and Erin, along with chocolate chip cookies and fresh fruit cups. "I left the sandwiches and salads in the refrigerator to stay cold as long as possible."

I nod. "Good idea. We'll have them for supper." I find myself loitering in the open doorway between my office and the nursery, not wanting to put too much distance between myself and my baby. He's sound asleep in his crib, and he's plenty warm, but I can't help worrying.

I check my phone to see if I've missed any texts from Shane, but there's nothing new. I had expected him to contact me again, but he seems to have gone radio silent. I'm sure he's busy dealing with his own crises at the McIntyre Building. I wonder if all his employees were able to head home before the Level Three snow emergency was issued.

"What's wrong?" Sam says.

Startled, I jump. "Nothing. I'm just surprised I haven't heard anything more from Shane. Do you think he's mad at me? For not going home when I had the chance?"

Sam chuckles as he pulls me into his arms. "He's not mad at you. He could never be mad at you. He's probably busy, and a bit worried. They both are."

And by *both*, I know he means Cooper, too. "I miss Shane."

Sam hugs me gently, running his hand up and down my back. "I know you do. And I'm sure he misses you more. Honestly, he's probably going apeshit right now, knowing you and Luke are stranded here and he's not with you. *News flash*—Mack has been sending him regular updates via text, so Shane knows our power is out. But he also knows you and Luke are safe."

Erin returns to my office with her arms full of fleece blankets and small novelty pillows. "At least we won't freeze to death," she says, as she dumps the goods on the sofa.

"Come on, princess," Sam says, pulling me by the hand to the sofa. "Sit down and relax for a while. We'll hear Luke if he wakes up."

The three of us crash on the long sofa, putting our feet up on the coffee table. My arms feel conspicuously empty without my baby, and I almost wish he'd wake up so I'd have an excuse to hold him.

When my phone rings, I sit up, eagerly reaching for it, hoping it's Shane. But it's not. It's my brother. "Hi, Tyler!"

His deep voice comes across the phone line loud and clear, and he sounds very much like the police detective he is as he peppers me with questions. "Beth, where are you? Where's Luke? What's your situation? Are you somewhere safe?"

"We're fine. We're at Clancy's."

The line goes silent for a moment, and I start to think the call was dropped. But then Tyler blows out a harsh breath, his tone gently chiding. "You should be at home, Beth."

"Believe me, I wish I was. But don't worry. Sam and Mack are here with us, so is Erin, plus two other security guards. We'll be fine. We've lost power, but the generators are running the emergency lights. And hopefully the building will retain most of its heat until the power comes back on."

"Where's Shane?"

"He's at his office building, with Cooper. They're both stranded there."

"I'd come get you, but the streets are hazardous right now. You're much better off hunkering down there and waiting for the streets to clear."

"Are you at home?"

"Yes. Don't worry about me."

"What about Mom?" I say. "Have you talked to her? Where is she?"

"She's fine. Bridget and Calum invited her to stay with them until this storm blows over. Jake's right next door to them, so if they need anything, he can help them."

Mentally, I start going down the list, wondering where everyone in our family is. I'm grateful to Shane's parents for taking my mother into their home during this storm. My mom recently moved into a small, single story home in what we're now affectionately calling 'the McIntyre family compound.' Her home is right next door to Lia and

Jonah's new house, and across the street from Bridget and Calum's house. I'm sure they're all worried about their kids and grandkids. Lia and Jonah are surely safe and sound at home. But what about Shane's sister Sophie? And what about Molly and Jamie? And Liam? I hate this!

"Save your phone battery," my brother says. "Use it sparingly."

"I will. Mack has portable battery chargers, so we're okay there."

"Good. Stay indoors. Call me if there's an emergency and I'll find a way to get to you. Be safe, okay?"

"I will. Thank you. You be safe, too. I love you."

My brother is very stern and controlling, but he's also very caring. He's always watching out for me, and for his nephew now, too. He and Shane lock horns quite a bit, but that's understandable. They're both strong-willed men who feel responsible for protecting the people they love.

Ironically, it was Tyler who introduced me to Shane, indirectly at least. My brother hired McIntyre Security to protect me when my childhood abductor was released from prison. I suspect that Tyler has regretted that decision a time or two. Like the time he had Shane thrown in jail on trumped up charges of physically assaulting an officer, when it was Tyler who threw the first punch. Shane was just defending himself.

An hour later, I receive a call from Joe. He tells me he got Kayla safely to the hospital, and then on his way back here, to get us, he was stopped by the police and given a citation for driving illegally during a Level Three snow emergency. I tell him to go home, back to the apartment building we all share, to wait out the storm.

One hour morphs into two as the afternoon drags on. I'm listening for Luke to wake up. He's going to be hungry soon. I know it's nearly time to nurse him again because my breasts feel heavy with milk.

I still haven't heard anything more from Shane, and it's wearing on my nerves. I've texted him twice and tried calling him a couple of times, but I received no answer. *Is he mad at me? Is something wrong at his office building?* It's not like him to go radio silent. I try not to read too much into it, but it's eating at me.

I try another text:

Shane? Is everything okay?

"What are you doing?" Sam says, bumping my shoulder with his.

The three of us are on the sofa, Sam on my left and Erin on my right. The room has definitely cooled off since we lost power, but the fleece blankets are doing their job.

"Texting Shane again. He's not responding."

"I haven't heard anything more from Cooper either. They must be busy. They're probably fielding all kinds of urgent requests at work."

"I suppose so."

When Luke's sleepy cries filter through the open nursery door, Sam stands. "I'll get him."

Sam disappears into the nursery, and I follow him, needing something to do to take my mind off worrying about Shane. Luke is sitting up in his crib, a bit wobbly as he's not fully awake. He rubs his eyes with tiny fists, blinking as he adjusts to the lights.

Sam holds his hands out to Luke, and Luke reaches for him. "Mum-mum."

"Hey, little guy," Sam says as he carries Luke to the changing table and pulls out a fresh diaper. I watch as Sam changes Luke's diaper, smiling when Sam blows raspberries on Luke's belly, making him giggle until he's breathless. There's nothing sweeter than the sound of a baby's laughter.

Sam's so good with Luke. He and Cooper would make wonderful parents. "Do you want kids of your own?" I ask him.

"I'd like to have kids, yeah. And I think Cooper would be up for having kids—just look at how he's adopted you. But I've got to get him to walk down the aisle with me first. One step at a time, I guess."

I watch as Sam redresses Luke, who's more awake now, his eyes bright as he watches me and then Sam, and me again.

"Mum-mum!" Luke says, grinning at me as he kicks his legs.

"I'll bet you're hungry," I say, reaching out to hold his hand. My arms are itching to hold my son, but I force myself to relax. *Relax. Luke's perfectly fine. We're all fine.* I repeat my mantra over and over in my head because the last thing I need is to have a panic attack.

Sam zips up Luke's PJs and lifts him into a standing position, supporting Luke as he tries to put his feet on the changing table's padded surface. "It's getting chilly," he says. "I think we should keep him in his sleeper. It'll be warmer for him."

Luke reaches for me with a whimper. I take him in my arms, settling him on my hip, and he clutches my sweater.

He reaches with his free hand for a wayward strand of hair that has fallen from my ponytail. "Mum-mum-mum!" Then he lays his head on my chest.

"Someone's hungry," Sam says, heading for the door to give us some privacy. "You feed the peanut. I'll keep Erin company."

* * *

An hour later, Erin and I are seated alone on the sofa. Sam took Luke with him downstairs to visit with Mack.

Erin rests her head on the back of the sofa and turns to look at me. She looks a bit weary. "How long do you think we'll be stuck here?"

I shrug. "Just until morning, I hope. Then the streets will begin to clear—once it's light outside and the snow plows can make a path for the tow trucks to get in here and start removing these cars." I reach over and squeeze her hand. "Don't worry."

Erin has already called her roommates to let them know she wouldn't be coming home this evening. All three of the other girls are safe in their apartment in Rogers Park. Their university closed at noon because of the snow. Erin nods, giving me a weak smile. Then she stands and heads to the snack table to survey our meager options. She picks up a pint-sized, clear plastic container of fresh cut fruit and a plastic fork. "Do you want one?"

"Sure. I don't think I've eaten anything healthy today."

She hands me a fruit cup and a fork, then gets one for herself. "My roommates are organizing a New Year's Eve party," she says. "It's going to be held at the Wakefield Hotel bar."

"Nice. Are you going?"

She shrugs. "I don't know. I'm not much of a partier, but I thought it would be fun to go out and do something social for a change. Especially on New Year's Eve."

She pauses, eyeing me, and I can tell there's something more she wants to say. Erin is the quintessential wallflower simply because she's *so* shy. She and I are alike in so many ways—we're both such introverts—and I think that's why we've become such good friends. Erin is twenty-two, and I don't think she's ever had a drink in her life. "There will probably be lots of drinking at this party," I tell her.

"Well, it is a New Year's Eve party, at a *bar*. That usually entails drinking."

It doesn't sound like something Erin would enjoy doing, but if she wants to do it, she certainly can. She's old enough. "If you really want to go, then go."

"The other girls are bringing dates."

Ah. That's what this is about.

Very casually, too casually, she says, "I thought about asking Mack."

"You should ask him."

"I'm sure he'll say no." She sounds so dejected, and perhaps for good reason. She's asked Mack to do things before, and he's always said no.

"It won't hurt to ask him," I say.

It's no secret that Erin has been crushing on Mack Donovan ever since Shane assigned him as head of store security. I have my suspicions that her interest isn't entirely one-sided. The problem is that Mack is thirty-five, and he's seen and done a lot during his stint in the military, whereas Erin has lived such a sheltered life. She's never even had a boyfriend. Shane has made it abundantly clear to Mack that he'd better keep his distance from Erin, or he'll have to answer to Shane.

I think Shane's exact words were, "*Keep your God damned hands off Erin O'Connor, or you'll fucking answer to me.*" And Shane was serious. Thinking about Shane makes me wonder what he's doing, and why he hasn't contacted me lately. I send him another text, asking if everything's all right, but he doesn't reply.

Just as I remove the lid from my container of fruit, we hear a shattering of glass coming from outside the store. We both jump to our feet and race to look out the window. Visibility is still poor, but we can make out the several figures dressed in dark clothing, their faces obscured by dark ski masks, moving on the street. One of them swings a sledgehammer at the front driver's window of an SUV, shattering the glass. They're breaking into the stranded vehicles, pilfering around inside for anything of value. Car alarms are going off left and right, the noise a muffled cacophony of shrill and jarring sounds.

Erin looks even paler than usual as we watch two of the masked individuals change direction and head toward our side of the street. She looks horrified. "What if they try to break into the store?"

"Luke's downstairs!" I cry, practically choking on the words. The air leaves my lungs in an explosive rush, and I'm racing for the door, with Erin right behind me.

4

Beth McIntyre

Erin and I run out of my office and down the hall to the staircase that leads to the main floor below. Sam's already halfway up the stairs, a sobbing baby clutched tightly in his arms.

He shoves Luke into my arms. "Take him and get back upstairs!"

I nod. But Erin has already raced past us, down the stairs as she heads straight to Mack, who's standing directly in front of the doors.

"Erin, wait!" I call after her. But she's not listening. "I can't leave her down here," I tell Sam as I push past him and go after Erin.

Clearly on alert, Mack has planted himself right in front of the inner set of glass doors. My heart sinks when I see that Mack has removed his jacket, presumably so that it's easier for him to access the handgun holstered to his chest.

The view outside Clancy's is surreal. The snow drifts high against the windows, blocking a great deal of our view of the sidewalk and street. Still, I can make out a number of dark figures lurking outside our doors.

Sam follows and wraps his arm around Erin's shoulders to draw her back a few yards from the doors. She's visibly upset.

Sam points her in my direction and gives her a gentle nudge. "You need to go back upstairs with Beth. Now."

We hear more glass shattering outside, more car alarms going off. Darkness is falling fast, and it's barely three in the afternoon. It's as if the laws of nature have taken the day off. My heart starts pounding, and my breath feels caged in my tight chest.

Mack gives me a long, considering glance, as if he's assessing my state of mind. Then he turns to Sam. "Take the girls upstairs."

Erin breaks away from Sam. "No! I'm not leaving you down here alone."

"I have a job to do, kiddo," Mack says, catching her when she reaches him. He gently brushes back her dark hair, his expression inscrutable as he bends down to face her. His lips press into a hard line as he looks away, back out at the street, and then back to Erin. "Honey, please."

Mack makes an imposing figure, dressed in black slacks and a black T-shirt with a white McIntyre Security logo on it. His shirt molds itself to his muscles, the ridges of his abdomen visible beneath the cotton fabric. At nearly six-and-a half feet tall, Mack towers over Erin's petite frame. He's solid, built like a tank. It's rare that I see him without his jacket on. His left arm is covered in a patchwork of dense, intricate tattoos visible below the short sleeve of his shirt.

He makes a striking picture standing there, hyperalert, yet distracted by Erin. He runs his long fingers through his short dark hair, then his hand slips down to brush his closely-trimmed beard. The unconscious gesture reminds me so much of Shane it hurts.

Mack Donovan is such a good man, through and through. I hurt for Erin, knowing how she feels about him, and knowing that Mack won't allow himself to reciprocate those feelings. I hurt for both of them.

"She's too young, Beth," he's told me more than once. "It just wouldn't be right."

I know Mack's thinking about his own daughter, who's seventeen years old—just five years younger than Erin. During his senior year in high school, Mack and his then-girlfriend found themselves with a baby on the way. In the end, they decided not to marry. Instead, the girlfriend went on to college, and Mack joined the military.

The girl's mother has custody of their child, but Mack is very close to his daughter. He's always paid child support to the girl's mother, and ever since he returned to the states, he's seen his daughter a couple of times each week.

Technically, he's not old enough to be Erin's father. But he's thirty-five, and she's just twenty-two, and according to Shane, that's too wide of a gulf between them. But it's not just the age difference. It's the fact that Mack has lived a hard life. After over a decade in the military, having completed several rough tours in Iraq and Afghanistan, he's done and seen a lot of things, both in his professional life and in his personal life. And Erin... she's so innocent.

Erin thinks Mack doesn't have any feelings for her. I happen to know that's not true. I've seen the way he looks at her when she's not watching. The longing—the hunger—in his expression is obvious.

"Age is just a number, Mack," I've told him time and time again. *"Look at me and Shane. He's eleven years older than I am."* But that argument never seems to help.

Mack glances at me now, looking like he's in over his head. "A little help here, Beth?" he says, raising a beseeching brow. "I need you guys upstairs."

"Erin, please come back upstairs," I tell her, reaching for her hand. "I need your help with Luke."

She looks at me, obviously torn.

I know why Mack wants us upstairs. There's a panic room on the second floor, just a few doors down from my office. The room has specially reinforced walls and door. There are security monitors and emergency communication equipment inside. It even has its own emergency power source, so it's fully functional even in a crisis—like this blizzard.

I tug gently on her hand. "Erin, please. Come back upstairs with me. Let Mack do his job."

Erin looks so small standing next to Mack. With her pale complexion, bright blue eyes, and chin-length dark hair, she reminds me of a porcelain doll, or something out of a fantasy story.

I've never seen her this emotional, or this demonstrative, around

Mack. Usually, she tries hard to keep her feelings to herself and not wear her heart on her sleeve. And inadvertently, she's just making this horrible situation even harder for Mack, who probably wants nothing more than to take Erin upstairs himself and keep her safe.

Erin is so conflicted as she's pulled between the two of us. She's loyal to a fault, and I hate manipulating her like this. She looks up at Mack, then at me.

Mack turns back to face the doors and the chaos lurking outside, clearly dismissing Erin. "Get upstairs, Erin," he snaps. "Now!"

Erin winces, clearly hurt by Mack's brusque tone of voice.

Sam puts an end to the discussion by taking hold of Erin's shoulders and pointing her toward the stairs, giving her a gentle push as he marches her toward the steps. "Come on, Erin. Time to go."

I follow them up the stairs, trying to placate a crying infant. When we reach the second floor, I pull Erin close for a one-armed hug. "Come on. Let's go back to my office."

"He shouldn't be down there all by himself," she whispers, her expression pained.

Sam escorts us back to my office.

"Those men came right up to our doors," she says. "They acted like they were going to break the glass with a sledgehammer, but when they saw Mack, they backed off. But they're still out there! And they know we're in here."

Sam gives Erin a look. "I told you, we're sitting on a ton of cash right now. That's a pretty big inducement."

A chill runs down my spine at the thought of those faceless men breaking into my bookstore and threatening us. I don't care one bit about the money, but if any of my friends got hurt... I can't even contemplate it. "Mack will keep them out," I tell her, sounding a lot more sure than I feel. Mack is grossly outnumbered down there.

Erin and I retreat to my office, along with Sam, who shuts the door behind us. Sam seems antsy, preoccupied, and I'm sure he's worrying about what's going on downstairs.

Luke has worked himself up to a good cry. I think the noise and tension is getting to him.

"It's okay, sweetie," I say, kissing his forehead. I drop down onto the sofa, pulling one of the fleece blankets over my shoulder, and unbutton my blouse. Luke latches on eagerly, more for comfort than because he's actually hungry. I rub his back and he quiets.

Erin retrieves her fruit cup from the table and joins me on the sofa, and Sam moves to the window, keeping watch on the sidewalk and street below. I know he wants to go downstairs to help Mack, but at the same time, he's reluctant to leave us.

I catch his gaze. "You can go, Sam. It's okay."

Sam shakes his head. "I'm not leaving you girls to fend for yourselves. If there's a breech down below, we'll evacuate to the panic room."

His statement makes me feel sick, because a breech downstairs means that Mack has been overpowered. And I know Mack wouldn't go down without a fight, so that entire scenario is out of the question. If the looters make it inside the store... My God, I can't even think about what that would mean for Mack.

Erin grows even paler as she sinks back onto the sofa and wraps one of the blankets around herself.

I give Sam a look. *Stop scaring her!* "Go, Sam. Mack needs you more than we do."

He's clearly torn, but he knows I'm right. Guarding the doors and keeping the criminal elements out has got to be the priority. "All right," he finally concedes. Then he shakes a finger at me. "But if you hear *anything*, and I do mean *anything*, you run for the panic room. Do you hear me? Lock yourselves in there and sit tight until I, or someone you trust, comes to let you out."

I nod, trying not to imagine the worst.

"Do you promise?" he says, looming over me with a stern expression. "No heroics, from either of you. You have to promise me."

"Yes," we say in unison. "We promise."

৫ 5

Beth McIntyre

L uke falls asleep in my arms. Erin asks if she can hold him, and I hand him over to her, knowing that he'll help keep her mind off what's going on downstairs.

I make a quick run to the ladies' room, and then come back to stand at the window and observe the street. I count five individuals dressed in dark clothing, their faces obscured by hoodies and masks. I think they're all men, but it's impossible to be sure. They systematically shatter car windows and take whatever they can find from inside the vehicles.

After a while, the masked looters congregate behind an abandoned Mercedes coupe, deep in discussion. Then, sledgehammers in hand, they approach our side of the street, heading for the jewelry store to our left. The sound of plate glass shattering is loud and jarring.

Erin flinches. "Shouldn't we go to the panic room?"

I shake my head and battle a hot wave of nausea. My pulse is racing, and I feel queasy. "They're breaking into the jewelry store next door."

Even from my office, we can hear the jewelry store's alarm system going off. God, I hope no one is in there.

"This is unreal," Erin says, gently rocking the sleeping baby in her arms.

For a moment, I imagine Erin holding a dark-haired baby of her own. I imagine Mack becoming a father for the second time. He'd have an almost-adult daughter and an infant.

"It is unreal," I say, trying to keep my mind on what Erin's saying.

For a moment, I let my mind wander, thinking about Shane and what he might be doing right now. I'm sure he's not a happy camper, separated from us. I miss him terribly, the longing an ache in my chest. At least he has Cooper with him.

Suddenly, two of the looters approach our doors. "Erin, they're coming our way."

Erin freezes and peers up at me from the sofa. "What do we do?"

One of the looters raises the sledgehammer in both hands and swings with all his might, making contact with one of our outer glass doors. The sound of glass shattering is unmistakable. Suddenly we hear shouting downstairs, from our guys. They're talking fast. I can't make out any of what they're saying, but it's clearly our signal.

"Let's go!" I tell Erin, as I take Luke from her. I swing the strap of Luke's diaper bag over my shoulder and grab Erin's hand, pulling her out of my office. We turn left and race down the hallway to the panic room.

The panic room door is unmarked, and if you didn't know it was here, you'd never guess. There's a small, unmarked electronic key-pad next to it. I punch in the access code with a shaky finger, and the door unlocks with a quiet snick. I push the door open, then nudge Erin inside, following behind her into the room and pushing the door shut with my foot. It locks automatically with a hissing sound, sealing us inside.

As soon as we enter the pitch black room, a couple of lights come on, triggered by our motion. "Here, hold Luke." I place my son in Erin's arms and head for the control panel on the wall near the door. Erin stands back, cradling a sleeping baby in her arms, as I flip on a couple of the lights.

Erin looks around the room, her eyes wide as she takes it all in. Shane didn't spare any expense. He wanted this room to be a comfortable safe haven, and it is. My husband had this room built especially for me, back when Howard Kline was stalking me and becoming more and more aggressive in his actions.

It's part control room and part studio apartment. Besides the desk with monitors and emergency communication equipment, there's a gun safe embedded in the wall. On the other side of the room is a large sofa, which pulls out into a full-sized bed, two padded armchairs, and a flatscreen TV. There's even a small kitchen with a table, fridge, sink, and microwave. Nonperishable food is stashed in a cupboard. And at the back of the room is a door that leads to a bathroom with a shower and toilet.

Some of the more recent additions include a baby crib, a diaper changing table stocked with diapers and wet wipes and other necessary baby paraphernalia, and a padded rocking chair.

We have everything we need.

Except for our friends and my husband.

I can't even let myself think that anything could happen to Sam or Mack or the rest of our security team.

"Here, sit down before you fall down," I say, directing Erin to the rocking chair.

Just waking up, Luke reaches for me with a pitiful wail. "Mum-mum-mum!"

"I know, baby, but Mommy's busy right now." It kills me to turn away from him, but I know what I have to do. Shane and Cooper have drilled this into me time after time. I go to the wall safe, punch in the access code, and open the door. Inside is a Glock, which I've been trained to use.

Cooper's primary job is managing the McIntyre Security private shooting range, where he assesses the shooting skills of employees and potential new hires. He's a former shooting instructor in the Marine Corps, and he trained me ad nauseum in the proper way to handle a semi-automatic handgun. I know the rules. I've trained for this, over and over, until Cooper was satisfied with my performance.

I know how to handle the gun. I know the safety rules. And I'm also a really good shot. My eye-hand coordination is very good—

to the pleasant surprise of both Cooper and Shane. But shooting at paper targets suspended from a wire at an indoor shooting range is very different from shooting at a human being—and God forbid that should ever happen. But I'll do whatever I have to do to protect my family and friends.

I grab a preloaded magazine and snap it in place. Then I rack the slide, loading a round into the chamber. Carefully, I lay the loaded gun on the desk, with the muzzle facing the locked door, and sit down, ready to grab it if necessary. If the wrong person comes through that door, I'll likely only have one chance to stop him before he has a chance to overpower me.

The panic room is well insulated, so we can't hear what's going on downstairs. Erin holds Luke against her shoulder, rocking him and patting his back as she tries to comfort him. Occasionally we turn to look at each other, but neither one of us says anything. We're both afraid for our friends downstairs, and not knowing what's going on is agonizing.

"Wait! The cameras!" I say, reaching to turn on the bank of monitors. The screens power up, showing us in real time what's being recorded on the CCTV cameras throughout the store. There are cameras focused on nearly every square foot of the store, from the back alley to the café, to the front doors and sidewalks out front.

"Here!" Two cameras focus on the front entrance of the store: one from the outside, showing the front doors, and one from inside the foyer—that space between the outer glass doors and the inner doors.

My heart slams into my chest when I see two figures wielding sledgehammers step through the shattered outer door.

"Oh, crap!" I say. It's only a matter of time before they shatter the inner doors and gain access to the store.

Erin comes to stand behind me, watching over my shoulders at the tense stand-off downstairs. Mack and Sam are squaring off against the looters. They haven't drawn their guns yet, and I know they won't unless they fully intend to use them. The looters are posturing, their body language threatening as they debate whether or not to test our security forces.

When one of the looters takes a menacing step closer, raising the sledgehammer in his hands, Mack and Sam draw their guns in unison, holding them securely in both hands, their stances rigid as they send a warning message to the looters. If you break that door, we will shoot you.

The air is trapped in my lungs and I feel like I can't get a breath. My pulse races as tears obscure my vision. *This can't be happening!*

Erin leans closer to watch the drama unfolding downstairs. As if he can sense the tension in the room, Luke whimpers and reaches for me. But I can't hold him now. I'm sitting in front of a load handgun, pray I won't have to use it.

We can't hear what's going on down there, as there's no audio, but a moment later, it's clear that something's happening. The two looters in the foyer turn to look behind them, out onto the sidewalk, their stances tensing. Mack and Sam both lower their guns and straighten, their postures visibly relaxing. Sam tucks his handgun into the back waistband of his jeans as he watches through the doors. Mack holsters his.

The other camera—the one focused on the sidewalk in front of the store—shows another group of men descending on our location. They're dressed in cold weather gear, their faces fully covered, but their motives are clear. The new arrivals draw handguns on the looters, boxing them in. The looters drop their sledgehammers and put their hands on their heads. At first, I think it must be the police, but I don't see any official emblems on our rescuers' clothing.

Three of the new arrivals round up the looters and herd them away from the store, off camera to the left, in the direction of the jewelry store they've already broken into. The remaining four new arrivals step over the shattered glass in the foyer, clearly intending to come inside the store.

My heart climbs into my throat as I wonder what we have to deal with now. But I instantly relax when I see a smiling Mack unlock the door.

The man in front of the group reaches up to remove his ski mask, whipping it off and revealing a man with short, disheveled brown hair and electric blue eyes.

I gasp. "Oh, my God! It's Shane!"

6

Beth McIntyre

I stare transfixed at my husband's image on the live camera feed. His hair is mussed from wearing a ski mask, and his complexion is a deep, ruddy hue undoubtedly from a combination of exertion and the cold temperatures. But still, he's the most beautiful sight I can imagine.

He's here.

I'm suddenly overwhelmed with emotions, everything from relief to joy to the simple desire to feel his arms around me, his lips on mine. Warmth floods my chest, easing the crushing pressure, and I can finally take an easy breath.

Shane says something to Sam, and Sam gestures up the stairs, smiling.

He's looking for me.

Three men file in behind Shane, removing their ski masks and outer gear. The first man has a silver buzz cut and a trim salt-and-pepper beard.

"It's Cooper!" I tell Erin, glancing back at her with a smile.

Sam marches right up to him, and the two men stand face-to-face, lost in each other's gaze. They clasp each other tightly, and Sam laughs as Cooper grips the back of his neck and kisses him soundly on the lips.

Our guys are here! They must have walked for hours in the blustery, waist-deep drifts of snow and bone-chilling cold temperatures.

I'm not one bit surprised, though. This is Shane and Cooper we're talking about. They wouldn't let anything as mundane as a once-in-a-century blizzard stand in their way.

Two more men remove their ski masks and hoods. "Liam!" *Shane's youngest brother.* "And Miguel!" *My first bodyguard.* These people aren't just friends; they're family.

I sink back into my chair, overwhelmed with dizzying relief. Shane's here, and he brought a small army with him. Everything's going to be just fine.

At the sight of so many familiar and beloved faces, my throat tightens, thick with tears. I stand, taking Luke in my arms, and kiss his cheek. "Your daddy's here," I whisper, my voice shaking. *We're okay.*

We leave the panic room and head for the stairs. The moment

I reach the top step, Shane looks up and his gaze locks on me with laser precision.

My heart hammers in my chest at the sight of him, and my legs shake so badly, I don't trust myself to walk down the stairs carrying Luke.

But it's okay, because Shane is already racing up the stairs, coming right for us. The instant I feel his arms come around me, I burst into tears, and my sobbing upsets Luke, who starts crying too. We're both emotional train wrecks. Shane laughs softly as he steers us safely back from the steps. Then, careful not to crush his son, he sweeps us both into his arms, enveloping us in a protective embrace, his chilled hands running up and down my back. The fact that his arms are shaking tells me everything I need to know. *He was afraid for us.*

One of his hands goes to the back of my head, cradling it as he crushes his mouth to mine. Our lips collide, and we're both breathing hard. I gasp, overcome with a mixture of relief and longing so intense it's a physical pain. Hot tears scald my cheeks. "Shane."

His arms tighten around me. "It's okay. I'm here." *He knows.* He knows me so well. "You're okay," he breathes close to my ear. "You're both okay."

Shane pulls back and smiles down at me, grinning when he sees the tears streaming down my cheeks. He brushes my tears away, then leans forward to kiss me, his lips nudging mine apart for a deeper connection. His lips linger on mine for a long moment, until we're interrupted by a squalling infant who's caught between us.

Luke grabs hold of Shane's sweatshirt and tugs, cooing "Mum-mum-mum!"

Shane leans down to kiss his son's forehead. "Hey, little buddy," he says in a low voice as he gently brushes Luke's cheek with the pad of his thumb. "How are you doing? You had a bit of excitement today, didn't you?" When he cups the back of Luke's head in his protective palm, my throat tightens again.

Shane looks back over the balcony railing at the small crowd below. In a voice rough with emotion, he says, "Hey, guys, give me a few minutes with my family. Let's meet in the café in ten minutes so we can plan watch shifts for the night."

Shane turns to Erin, who's standing with us, her eyes teary. He squeezes her shoulder. "How are you holding up, Erin?"

"Fine. I'm so glad you're here."

"So am I," he says, as if that isn't a huge understatement.

* * *

Shane lays his arm across my shoulders and we head for my office. Once there, he shuts the door behind us, and it's just the three of us in the quiet, dimly lit room.

"You must be exhausted," he says, shedding the rest of his winter gear. He hangs his coat from a hook on the back of the door.

"I am." I don't know what time it is, but it's fully dark outside. It's probably only around six o'clock—still early yet, but it feels like midnight to me.

Shane holds out his hands for Luke. I hand him the baby, and he holds Luke in the air so he can look him over from head to toe.

Luke smiles at his daddy and kicks his legs eagerly.

"Mum-mum-mum-mum-mum."

"Well, aren't you talkative today," he says, grinning.

I laugh. "He's been very talkative today. Everything is 'mum-mum-mum.'"

Shane smiles at his son. "Say *da-da*."

"Mum-mum-mum."

Shane props Luke on his hip, holding him close, as he pulls me into another embrace. His voice is low and a bit rough when he says, "Jesus, all I could think about was getting here to you two." He tightens his hold on me and lets out a heavy sigh.

"I'm so glad you're here." Now that the initial shock of seeing Shane has passed, my entire body is shaking.

"You need to rest," he says. "You look like you're about to keel over."

I laugh because he's right. My legs could give out on me at any time. "I think the stress has gotten to me."

"We'll crash in the panic room," he says. "We can make up the sofa bed, and there's a crib in there for Luke. Why don't you guys go get comfortable in there while I go downstairs to talk with the guys. I'll let someone else take the first shift so I can stay with you and Luke a while longer."

I slip my arms around his waist. "We're going downstairs with you." I lean into him and go up on my toes to kiss the side of his throat, right over his pulse point. "I want to stay with you."

He tightens his hold on me and kisses me once more, his lips lingering on mine for a long moment. "Okay." Then he shifts his grip on Luke and takes my hand. "Let's go."

* * *

It's a little chaotic downstairs in the café. Shane's guys are already raiding the refrigerated case for sandwiches and cold drinks. Fortunately, the fridge is well insulated, so the items are still pretty cold. I wish I could offer them some hot food, but cold sandwiches, chips, cookies, salads, and fruit will have to do.

We end up pushing several tables end-to-end so we can all sit together. Everyone gathers around the table except for Liam and Miguel, who are guarding the front doors, and the two other store security guys, Paul and Doug, who are still watching the rear alley entrance and the loading dock.

Shane grabs sandwiches for us while I carry cold drinks to the table.

"We need to set up shift rotations," Shane says, once he's seated beside me. He takes a bite of his sandwich. He's balancing Luke on his thigh, and the baby tries to reach for Shane's food.

I reach into the diaper bag for a jar of pureed peas and pop the lid. When he sees me holding a baby spoon, Luke reaches for me, a big grin on his sweet little face. "Mum-mum-mum."

The guys start planning who's taking which shift, and for how long. Then they discuss who's going to crash where for some much-needed sleep. Fortunately, there are padded benches throughout the store, and plenty more fleece blankets. Also, there's my office upstairs, the nursery, and the panic room. There are enough makeshift surfaces that folks can crash on and get some much needed rest.

"Sam and I will take the next watch at the front doors," Cooper says, taking charge. "Mack, you and your guys need to rest. You've been on duty all day. Liam and Miguel will watch the rear doors. We'll rotate on four-hour shifts. Everybody eat up and get to it. Shane, you go upstairs with your family."

Shane nods, taking the baby spoon from me so he can feed Luke. "Thanks."

"I can take a shift," Erin says, her gaze bouncing from Cooper to Shane and finally settling on Mack.

"No!" all three men say in unison.

"That won't be necessary, young lady," Cooper says, gentling his tone. "You need to rest, darlin'. You've had a long, stressful day."

Exhaustion is catching up with me, and I can barely keep my eyes open. It's not that late in the evening, probably only seven o'clock, but after the insane day we've had, my body is crashing.

Shane watches me closely. "Are you okay, sweetheart?"

I nod. "Just tired."

"We're going upstairs," he says to everyone seated at the table. "Beth and I will commandeer the panic room. Erin can take the sofa in the nursery, and Sam and Cooper can have the sofa in Beth's office. The rest of you, crash wherever you can find a comfortable spot."

Erin looks as exhausted as I feel. She nods gratefully at Shane, and then her gaze flits momentarily to Mack.

Mack doesn't look one bit tired. In fact, he looks like he's raring to go for another shift. But he has to be exhausted. As our first line of defense, he bore the brunt of the stress all day.

Shane stands, taking Luke from me so I can collect his bowl and spoon. He checks his phone, then nods to Cooper. "I'll relieve you at 2300 hours."

Erin accompanies us up the stairs, and we drop her off at my office, then continue on to the panic room. Shane punches in the access code and opens the door. As we step inside, he pauses when he sees the loaded Glock lying on the desk. He gives me a look of quiet reprimand and hands me Luke, while he retrieves the gun, removes the magazine and the round in the chamber, and stows the gun in the wall safe.

"Beth, sweetheart, don't ever leave a loaded gun lying around," he says, his tone gently chiding.

"I'm sorry. When I saw it was you downstairs, I raced out of here and forgot all about the gun."

"It won't be long before Luke's walking," he says, not stating the obvious.

Shane refrains from reading me the riot act. If Cooper were here, he wouldn't hesitate to lecture me. When it comes to guns, there are rules to be followed. Period. No excuses.

Shane sits Luke in his high chair and hands him some toys. Then, to me, he says, "Why don't you grab some sheets and pillows while I pull out the bed."

The sofa bed unfolds into a comfortable full-sized bed. I return with sheets, a heavy blanket, and two pillows, and we make up the bed together.

Luke reaches for me, starting to fuss. He's tired, too, but he wants to nurse before sleeping.

"I'll get him ready for bed," Shane says, "while you get yourself ready."

I head for the bathroom to freshen up, and when I return, Shane and Luke are already in bed. Shane's clothes are folded neatly and draped over a chair. He's lying bare chested, the bedding up to his waist. I stand staring at him for a moment, mesmerized by the way his arm muscles flex as he plays a game of tug-of-war with Luke.

When Luke sees me, he quickly loses interest in the game and reaches for me. "Mum-mum-mum," he says, pouting.

Shane grins at me as he brushes the top of Luke's downy head. "I don't blame you, son. I want to cuddle with her, too. But it looks like I'll have to wait my turn."

I smile as I undress, leaving on only my bra and panties. The air is chilly after a number of hours with no heat in the building, so I eagerly slip beneath the bedding to warm up. Luke lunges toward me, and I catch him.

I lie down, my head on my pillow, and roll onto my side to face Shane. While I'm positioning Luke, Shane reaches over to unhook one of the cups of my bra. I'm so tired I can barely stay awake. Lulled and comforted by the gentle tug on my breast, I close my eyes and allow myself to relax for the first time all day. Shane talks quietly to Luke as he strokes my hair.

Just as I'm dozing off, I jump reflexively, waking with a start.

"It's okay, you can sleep," Shane says, brushing his thumb across my forehead. "We have a small, yet highly competent army downstairs guarding this fortress. There's nothing to worry about."

7

Shane McIntyre

As I watch my son fall asleep at his mother's breast, I'm swamped with emotion. I'm in awe of the baby we created. I'm in awe of my wife. And I'm scared shitless by how much they both mean to me. Earlier today, when I realized the danger that was unfolding as a result of the storm, I nearly had a panic attack of my own.

Knowing that Beth and Luke were stranded here was more than I could bear. All I could think about was getting to them. I would have trudged through waist-high snow drifts for days to get to them, if that's what it took.

Cooper and I, along with my brother Liam, Miguel, and several others still in the McIntyre Security building bundled up in arctic survival gear and set off on foot for Clancy's. There was no point trying to take a vehicle. Even without the Level Three Snow Emergency, the streets were choked with snow and stranded cars.

It took us hours to make the three-mile trek, mostly because we stopped at each abandoned car to make sure no one was trapped inside or injured. We did come across one young family with two children who were essentially trapped in their car because none of them was adequately dressed for the weather. Two of our guys ended up taking them back to the office building so they could wait out the storm in comfort and safety.

But I kept going, as did Cooper, who was just as anxious to get to Sam as I was to get to Beth. Even though Sam is a well-trained—and well-armed—bodyguard, who's perfectly capable of taking care of himself in any situation, he's still Cooper's boyfriend, and that changes everything.

My heart about stopped when we reached the bookstore just as two assholes with sledgehammers were threatening to break down the front door. Mack and Sam both stood steadfast at the doors, armed and ready to defend their fortress against the trespassers.

We got there just in time. Another few minutes more, and Mack and Sam would have been forced to shoot. I have no doubt they would have prevailed, but it would have been an unfortunate, and unnecessary, loss of human life.

My guys apprehended the looters and took them into the jewelry store next door—which had already been looted—to hold them secure with handcuffs until the police could apprehend them and charge them for all the destruction they'd perpetrated.

At that point, all I wanted to do was get inside Clancy's and find my wife and son. I knew I wouldn't be able to rest easy until I had them in my arms.

The relief on Mack's and Sam's faces when we arrived was palpable. I think they were literally moments away from pulling their triggers and ending the lives of a bunch of unruly yahoos.

Luke relaxes in sleep, his slack mouth falling away from Beth's nipple. I cover Beth to keep her warm and carry Luke to the crib. Once he's safely in his crib, I make use of the restroom, then return to bed so I can cuddle with my wife.

Beth is out like a light when I crawl under the bedding and pull her into my arms. Her skin is chilled, so I roll her to her side, facing away from me so I can spoon against her back, my arm tucked around her waist. The heat of my body will keep her plenty warm.

With a soft sigh, she presses back against me, immediately making me harden. God, even after all the time we've been together, I don't think she fully realizes the effect she has on me.

Being this close to her, smelling the scent of her skin, of her hair, makes me hard. I try to ignore my erection, which is pressed against her soft, rounded buttocks. But that's easier said than done. I press my face against the back of her head, breathing her in and telling myself to be satisfied with just holding her.

My cock is aching for a more intimate connection, but that's going to have to wait. She's exhausted and slightly traumatized by the day's events. Right now she needs rest and comfort, not a randy husband to deal with.

I'm too wired to sleep right now—not to mention far too aroused—so I content myself with just holding her. The cup of her nursing bra is unfastened, and I slip a hand inside to cup her breast, loving the feel of that soft, heavy weight in my hand. I brush the nipple with my thumb and smile when a drop of warm moisture beads on my skin.

She stirs in her sleep, a soft sound escaping her as she rolls toward me. "Luke? Is he—"

"He's asleep in his crib. Go back to sleep, sweetheart."

She hugs my arm to her chest, and I groan as my balls begin to ache with arousal.

God, I want more.

I slip a leg between hers, my thigh pressed against the wet heat of her pussy, and grit my teeth as my dick hardens. I want to sink deep inside her. I want to feel her muscles contracting around my cock, squeezing me. But now's not the time.

Instead, I lay my cheek against the top of her head and close my eyes with a heavy sigh.

* * *

I figure a couple hours have passed when Beth stirs in my arms. She comes awake with a start, and I tighten my arms around her. "It's okay. I'm here. Everything's fine."

Her eyes flash wide open in the semi-darkness as she peers around the unfamiliar room. I'm glad I left a nightlight on in the bathroom because I didn't want her waking up in a strange place in complete darkness.

"Where's Luke?" she asks in a slightly panicked voice.

"He's asleep in his crib."

I haven't slept a wink—I'm way too wired to sleep.

The bedding has slipped down, exposing her bare back, and she shivers.

"Here," I say, tucking the blankets around her. I reach beneath the bedding and rub her back, warming it with my hand.

"Mmm," she moans in pleasure as she burrows closer to me, her arm slipping around my waist. "I was so happy to see you this evening," she murmurs in a quiet, sleepy voice. "I was worried when you stopped texting me."

"I'm sorry. It was a rough trek getting here. And it was too cold to take our phones out. I was focused on getting here as quickly as possible. I was afraid there might be looters out, and a store this big would have a lot of cash on hand after an event like today."

"Are you mad at me?"

I pull back so I can see her face. "Mad at you? Why would you think that?"

"For insisting that Joe take Kayla to the hospital. I missed my ride home."

"Sweetheart." I sigh. "You did what you had to do. Yes, I wanted you and Luke home, but I understood. I might not have liked it, but I know you made the right call."

"What time is it?" she says.

I reach for my phone to check the time. "It's 2230 hours."

She laughs. "In English, please."

"Ten thirty. My shift starts in half an hour." I hate the idea of leaving her, even for a few hours, but duty calls.

"It feels so much later. My internal clock is out of whack." She turns to me and lifts her face to kiss the base of my throat, below my beard. "It'll be Christmas in an hour and a half."

I smile. "It's not exactly how you expected to spend your holiday, is it?"

She shakes her head. "Not exactly. I hope we can still make it to your parents' house for Christmas dinner tomorrow."

"We'll do our best."

"I hope so. It's Luke's first Christmas, and it's Aiden's first Christmas with your family. I don't want to miss that."

Beth begins tracing little circles on my back, her finger dipping lower with each pass. When her finger brushes the base of my spine, my nerve endings ignite, ratcheting up my simmering need. I can already feel my blood heading south and my dick beginning to throb as it swells. "Sweetheart, be careful. You're waking up the rocket."

She chuckles whenever I use that line from one of her favorite songs. "Maybe I want to wake it up." And then she trails kisses down the center of my chest. Her lips leave behind a trail of fire, heating my skin and scorching my nerves. With every teasing caress, I grow harder, my dick throbbing with pulsing need.

I suck in a harsh breath when she kisses her way across my pec to a nipple, flicking it with the tip of her tongue. I groan low in my throat. "Are you sure? You're exhausted, honey."

"I'm sure." She reaches up to kiss my throat, her lips pressing against my pulse point, which is beating fiercely. I groan, a little too loudly this time.

"Shh." She laughs softly. "You'll wake Luke."

"Heaven forbid," I say, rolling her to her back and looming over her. "That's it," I whisper hotly in her ear. "The rocket is fully awake now." Then I drink in her sighs, covering her mouth with mine as I nudge her lips open.

$\backsim$ 8

Beth McIntyre

Shane kisses me so thoroughly, so exquisitely that I feel an answering pull deep in my core. I feel myself growing hot and soft with each tug of his lips, each stroke of his tongue. His hand slips down between us, his fingers parting the lips of my sex and sliding through the lush wetness.

I used to fear this. I used to fear having him on top of me, caging me in and holding me down. It's taken a lot of time and patience on his part to help me get past the haunting memories of my childhood.

When I was just six, Howard Kline abducted me in broad daylight from my own front yard and kept me from my family for hours. I was left bound and naked in a cold, wet cellar in pitch darkness, but before he could do more to hurt me, the Chicago police department raided his property and rescued me.

My own brother, who was a rookie street cop at the time, was the first one to descend those cellar steps to save me. In hind sight, I realize how lucky I was. It could have been so much worse. And yet the emotional trauma from that nightmare has lasted almost two decades, affecting nearly every aspect of my life. It certainly affected my capability for intimacy.

But now, I revel in his weight on me. I take comfort in the feeling of his muscular arms holding me close.

He trails kisses along my jawline, down my throat, and I shiver when I feel his warm breath tickle my bare shoulder.

Without looking, he reaches for the front clasp of my bra and releases it, freeing both breasts from their confinement. With one hand, he cups a breast, while he nuzzles the other, finally latching onto my nipple, drawing it into his mouth and sucking gently. My breast aches as my milk starts flowing in an automatic response to the stimulation. He releases my nipple and licks, then trails kisses to the center of my chest, and then down my abdomen and belly.

Shane slips a finger inside the waistband of my panties. "These are in the way." Then he presses his nose to the fabric, right against my mound, and breathes in deeply with a low growl.

Rising up on his knees, he peels my panties down my legs and tosses them aside. Then he positions my legs, bent at the knees, and presses them apart so he can kneel between them. For a moment, he just looks at me, his hands gripping my knees hard, his eyes glittering with heated arousal as they take in my sex. He leans down and kisses the tender skin just above my mound, then drags his nose down, through the tufts of hair, until he reaches my clitoris. A simple flick of his hot tongue has my back bowing off the bed, and I gasp in pleasure.

He glances up at me, grinning, looking mightily pleased with himself. "Shh," he whispers. "Don't wake the baby."

It's so unfair, because I'm noisy when he goes down on me. I can't help it. It's just too much to take quietly. And he's so darn good at it. He teases and torments me relentlessly, never faltering, to the point I see stars when my body explodes in a mind-numbing orgasm. I press my lips closed, swallowing my own cries, and end up biting my lips and grasping at the sheets. But this time, he surprises me. Just when I'm on the cusp of climaxing, he rears back and stands at the foot of the bed. He shucks off his boxer-briefs, freeing an erection that's so thick, so engorged, it defies gravity.

Shane crawls between my legs and positions himself at my opening, pressing forward slowly as he sinks into me. Soft and wet, my opening welcomes him, drawing him inside. With his gaze locked onto mine, he rocks into me, then pulls back a bit, then rocks forward, a little deeper each time. When he's finally seated all the way, he leans down and wraps his arms around me, rolling us so that he's lying on his back and I'm sitting astride him, fully impaled on his erection.

"Is this okay?" he says, a bit breathless.

I nod, panting as my heart hammers in my chest.

He pulls me flush against his hips, and he's so deep inside I gasp.

Grasping my hips, he says, "I want you to make yourself come on me. I want to watch you."

My face heats, and I have to fight feeling self-conscious. He reaches up to cup the weight of my breasts, his thumbs brushing against my nipples, making them pucker. I think he likes the effects of nursing. My breasts are larger at the moment, heavier. His hands clamp down on my hips, which are noticeably wider now after pregnancy. From the way his fingers flex greedily on my flesh, I think he likes that too.

"Ride me," he murmurs in a voice that's deepened with arousal. "I want to watch you move, watch you find your pleasure." He slides his hands beneath my bottom and lifts me a bit, making me rock up on my knees, shifting the angle of penetration.

I gasp at the exquisite feeling of fullness. I love how he stretches me. When he's inside me like this, my entire world narrows down to him. I can't think of anything else.

"That's it, baby," he says. He raises his hips, pressing himself deeper inside me.

I bite my lip, the pleasure indescribable. He smiles when I moan helplessly.

I plant my palms on his broad chest, then lean forward a bit, gently rocking myself on him. Beneath my palms, I feel the low, rumbling growl deep in his chest. We're both trying so hard to be quiet and not wake the baby.

I'm so wet now, so slick, that I can move easily on him, rocking myself gently as I seek the right angle. I close my eyes and lose myself in pleasure as I rise and sink back down on him. I lean forward, changing the angle, searching until he hits me in just the right spot. When I find it, I gasp, biting down on my bottom lip to keep myself from keening like a banshee. *Oh, my God, right there. It feels so good.*

With my eyes closed, I can pretend he's not watching me, staring at me with so much hunger in his expression that his gaze is searing. I rock myself on him, faster and faster, riding him with longer strokes as I chase my orgasm. His hands return to my heavy breasts, and he brushes my nipples with his thumbs, making them tighten into hard little nubs. I swallow a cry.

"Open your eyes, sweetheart, and look at me. Let me watch you come."

His voice is so low and rough, like gravel, it sends shivers through me.

"Come on, baby. Look at me."

Reluctantly, I open my eyes, stunned by the fierce hunger in his. He looks like he wants to devour me whole.

I ride him shamelessly, the pleasure so exquisite. His shaft hits my sweet spot perfectly, and with each stroke, the tension in my body rises higher and higher.

He cups my face with his warm hands, making me look directly into his bright blue eyes. "God, I love you," he says with a groan. "Come on me, baby. Let me see you fly apart."

His voice, his words push me over the edge, and my body explodes, the walls of my vagina tightening on him, squeezing him hard. My gaze locks on his, and I can't look away. I cry out soundlessly, my breath heaving in my chest, and reach for his hands. Our fingers interlock, and we hold onto each other.

As soon as my orgasm wanes, he sits up, putting an arm around my back to hold me to him, and rolls us so that he's on top again. He rocks into me, hard and fast, moving easily in my slick channel as he chases his own climax. His mouth is hot on mine, our breaths mingling, our tongues seeking and stroking. He hammers into my wet heat, his chest heaving with harsh breaths.

Grasping my hands, he pins them to the bed beside my head, holding me fast as he drives into me. When his climax hits, he throws his head back, his neck muscles stretched taut, and grimaces silently, reining in his own hoarse cries. He bucks into me once, twice, and again, each time throbbing as he releases. Finally, he collapses on me, rolling us to our sides, and we lie quietly joined. When he releases my hands, I reach around him to stroke his back, soothing him as his erection continues to pulse inside me.

Brushing my hair from my damp face, he studies me. "Are you okay?"

My face heats with a blush. "I'm more than okay. I'm wonderful." It warms my heart that he never forgets to ask. Even though it's been a while since I've had an anxiety attack, he never takes it for granted.

Shane leans forward and kisses me gently. "I love you, Mrs. McIntyre."

My lips turn up in a blissful smile. "I love you, too, Mr. McIntyre."

He shakes his head, fighting a grin.

I smile at his reaction. "What's that for?"

Shane brushes the tip of his nose against mine. "I'm never letting you and Luke leave the house again, honey. My heart can't take it."

I know he's just making a joke, but underneath his words is a glimpse at just how worried he was today. I remember how his arms shook when he hugged me on the stairs earlier. *He was afraid for us.*

I reach over to brush his thick hair. "Sam and Mack were with us. We were never in any danger."

He raises an eyebrow. "If I recall correctly, my guys routed the pack of looters threatening your front door."

"Mack and Sam wouldn't have let them in. You know that."

He shrugs. "It was still too close for comfort."

* * *

After we both clean up in the bathroom, Shane settles me back into bed, tucking me in, and then he dresses.

"I'm going to check on things," he says. "And then I need to take a shift on guard duty. You go back to sleep. I'll come back to bed as soon as my shift is over." He leans down and kisses my forehead. "Text me if you need me." He kisses me once more, hesitating, as if he's reluctant to part from me. "I'll be back before you know it."

"It's okay. I'm fine. Go."

He nods, hesitating another moment. Then he turns and heads for the door. As he steps out, the door closes, and the programmed locks seal us in.

I roll onto my side and reach for his pillow. His scent is still on it, subtle, but comforting. I'll have to make do with that for now, until I have the real thing in my arms again.

9

Shane McIntyre

I hate leaving her, even for a few hours, but I have to go downstairs to spell Cooper and Sam. They've had a long day, too, and they need a little privacy and a chance to crash.

Even though Sam is perfectly capable of taking care of himself, Cooper still worries about him in times of duress. I think it's a natural reaction for any man to worry about the love of his life, even when his love is a six-foot tall, ex-Army Ranger who carries a 9 mm with him everywhere he goes.

I pause at the balcony railing and observe the main floor below. The store is quiet. The café is empty, and there's no sign of anyone up and about except for Sam and Cooper, who are sitting shoulder-to-shoulder, leaning against an interior wall as they face the front doors. They make a stunning pair, both dressed in jeans and flannel shirts, both wearing shit-kicker boots. From my vantage point, the only thing distinguishing them apart from each other is Cooper's buzzed silver cut and Sam's red manbun.

I'm happy for them both, and I'm damn proud of Cooper. I've known Cooper for a long time, dating back to our days together in the Marine Corps. I know how hard it was for him to come out this year and acknowledge his relationship with Sam. I wasn't sure he would ever take that step, but it was either that or risk losing Sam. And Sam won out.

Right now their fingers are interlaced, and their hands rest on Cooper's thigh. They're talking in low, hushed voices, and even though I can't hear what they're saying, I understand their meaning. When Cooper leans over and kisses Sam, his free hand gripping the back of Sam's head, the meaning is perfectly clear.

I head down the stairs, clearing my throat to make my presence known. Cooper stiffens and makes to release Sam's hand, but Sam holds on tight, refusing to unlink their fingers.

I come to stand right in front of them, my hands on my hips as I smile down at them with a mock salute. "Reporting for duty."

Cooper looks up with bloodshot blue eyes. "It's about time." He hauls himself to his feet and then reaches for Sam's hand, pulling him up too. "We're beat."

"Go crash." I laugh. "Good luck fitting the both of you on the sofa in Beth's office."

"Don't worry, we'll manage," Cooper says in a low, gravel voice. "How's our girl and my grandson?"

"Fine. Hopefully, they're both sound asleep."

"Good." Cooper nods. Then to Sam, he says, "All right, let's grab some food and head upstairs."

While those two raid the café, I do a quick sweep of the main floor, always keeping the front door in my sights.

I come across Mack in the history section, seated in a leather armchair with a Motocross magazine in his hands. Before I can ask him why the hell he's awake, when he should be sleeping, I notice a small figure across the way, curled up beneath a fleece blanket on a sofa in the romance section. Shoulder-length dark hair spills over a small pink pillow.

"What's Erin doing downstairs?" I say. "She could have slept on the sofa in the nursery."

"She was down here reading earlier and dozed off. I didn't have the heart to wake her, so I covered her with a blanket."

"And you felt the need to stand guard over her?" I can't help the heavy dose of skepticism in my voice. I know Mack has a very inappropriate interest in Erin O'Connor.

He raises his gaze to mine but doesn't say anything. He doesn't have to. We both know what he's thinking.

I've warned him time and time again to keep his distance from Erin. She's off limits to him. She's too young, too inexperienced. "Mack—"

He shakes his head curtly, his gaze narrowing on me. "Don't. I'm head of security here, and it's my job to keep the employees safe. I'd do it for anyone."

But it's not just anyone he's watching like a hawk. It's Erin. "Fine. Just don't cross the line, Mack. If you do, I'll reassign you in a heartbeat."

He clenches his jaws, but doesn't say anything. The muscle ticking in his cheek says it all.

* * *

I've got a four-hour wait until I can climb in bed with my wife again. *Four long hours.* I plant myself in easy view of the front doors and watch a whole lot of nothing going on outside on a frigid, blustery night. It's eerily dark outside since the power is off—none of the typical nighttime ambient light is present. I don't see any movement at all, unless you count blowing snow and shifting drifts.

I check in by radio with our guys next door who are holding the looters in custody until we can hand them over to the police. Liam and Miguel delivered some food and drinks to them earlier, to tide them over until the police arrive. It looks like our guys were able to recover the merchandise the looters had taken from the jewelry store—their pockets were jam packed with diamond jewelry and other precious gems.

Midway through my shift, I hear the faint sound of voices coming from the café. I glance in that direction to see Erin and Mack seated at a table for two, talking quietly. They both look exhausted. I wish Erin would go upstairs and sleep. But more than that, I wish she would get over her infatuation with Mack. She needs to find someone closer to her own age.

I realize I'm a bit of a hypocrite, as I'm considerably older than Beth, by almost as many years as separate Mack and Erin. But it was different for us. From the outset, almost as soon as I met her, I had every intention of marrying Beth. I don't know what Mack's intentions are, but I'm sure as hell not going to let him take advantage of an innocent young woman.

* * *

At three o'clock, my brother Liam comes down the stairs from the second floor, looking a little bleary eyed as he runs his fingers through his hair. Of all my brothers, he's the one who takes most after me, at least physically, with his brown hair and blue eyes.

"How's it going?" he says, as he offers me a fist bump.

I smile as I tap my knuckles to his. In so many ways, he reminds me of his twin, Lia. "Good." I stretch my neck and roll my shoulders, stiff from having sat in one position too long. "Everything's quiet outside. Hopefully you'll have a very boring shift."

Liam nods as he stretches his back and arms. "I hope to see some snow plows out on the street come day break. We need these streets cleared. Do you think we'll make it to Mom and Dad's for dinner?"

Our parents have planned a big family dinner at their new home later today—God, today is Christmas already. "I certainly hope so. Beth will be disappointed if we can't go."

"Not as disappointed as Mom will be. It's Luke's first Christmas—that's all she talks about. And Aiden is so excited he can't stand it."

"We'll do our best," I say. "That's all we can do."

I take my leave and head back up to the panic room, letting myself quietly into the room. After stripping down to my boxer-briefs, I climb onto the sofa bed, taking care not to wake Beth. Just as I lay my head on my pillow, I hear the tell-tale hum of the power coming back on in the building. Thank goodness the electricity has been restored. The building will be warm again by the time we awaken.

I press up against Beth to warm her slightly chilled body. Even with the covers on, she's a little cool. She sighs in her sleep as I slip my arm around her waist and draw her against me. I tuck my leg between hers and she moans softly.

"Shane?"

"Yes. Sorry if I woke you. Go back to sleep."

"What time is it?"

"A little after three."

"Is the power on? I thought I heard something."

"Yes. The power's back on."

"Good. I'm cold."

I tighten my arms around her as I bury my nose in her hair and breathe in her scent. "I'll warm you up."

"Thanks." She yawns sleepily. "Merry Christmas."

"Merry Christmas to you, too."

∞ **10**

Beth McIntyre

When I wake again, I'm toasty warm thanks to the oven plastered against my back. I stretch with a yawn, and Shane loosens his hold a bit. I have no idea what time it is, but my stomach tells me it must be time to get up and face the new day. I reach for my phone and check the time. Seven-fifteen.

Luke's awake, too. I can hear him moving around in his crib and talking to himself. Shane stretches beside me with a groan. It looks like we're all awake. When my stomach growls loudly, Shane chuckles.

"Somebody needs her breakfast," Shane says, going up onto his elbow so he can loom over me. He drops a kiss on the tip of my nose. "Good morning, wife."

With a smile, I reach up and brush his bearded cheek. "Good morning, husband."

"Mum-mum-mum."

We both glance over to see Luke sitting up in his crib, grasping the wooden bars with one hand, a small toy clutched in the other. "Mum-mum."

"That's my cue," I say, brushing my hair out of my face as I sit up. "Just a minute, sweetie. Mommy has to pee first."

Shane releases me after buzzing my cheek with a kiss. "I'll change him while you take care of business."

When I return from the restroom, Shane and Luke are in bed. Luke is happily climbing on Shane, but when he sees me, his priorities shift, and he reaches for me with a cry.

I laugh as I slip back into bed and reach for my son. "Come here, young man."

Shane watches his son eagerly latch onto my breast, and I rest my head on my pillow as my baby nurses. I rub Luke's back as he eats. Shane's hand is a warm, comforting weight on my hip.

I treasure moments like this, when it's just the three of us, together, quiet, just being a family. I can't help picturing a possible future in which another little face joins us, a little sister or brother for Luke, but Shane hasn't wanted to discuss having more children just yet. I think he's still recovering from Luke's delivery.

Shane's phone chimes softly, and he checks the screen. "Liam says the snow plows are out in full force now, working with the tow trucks to clear North Michigan."

"Thank goodness. Is the travel ban lifted?"

Shane does a quick search on his phone, checking the local news sites. "Yes. It's just a Level One now—*travel with caution*. So as soon as the road is cleared enough that Joe can get here with a vehicle, we can go home."

Halfway through nursing, I sit Luke up to burp him. He reaches for Shane, saying "Mum-mum-mum."

"How about *da-da*," Shane says.

Luke grins at him. "Duh."

Shane smiles. "Close enough." When Shane offers to pick him up, Luke lunges for me instead, lying down to resume nursing. Shane laughs. "I don't blame you one bit, pal."

"Oh, stop!" I say, laughing as I shift Luke so he can latch on to my other breast.

Another text message comes in to Shane's phone. "Mack says the police are en route to arrest the looters."

Once Luke is done nursing, I hand my son to his father so I can gather up my clothes and dress. "I need to check on Erin. I hope she was able to get some sleep last night."

"I saw her sleeping earlier on a sofa in the romance section."

"Downstairs? Well, at least she got some sleep."

"She did. And she had a guardian angel watching over her."

"Who?" I say, buttoning my blouse.

Shane gives me a look. "Who do you think?"

"Oh, Mack."

He nods. "Yes, Mack. I had another talk with him last night."

I frown. "I think you should back off and stop threatening Mack. He's a good guy, Shane. He'd never do anything to hurt Erin. Besides, aren't you being a bit of a hypocrite? Look at us."

"We're different. I was madly in love with you and had every intention of marrying you."

"Why do you assume they wouldn't be serious about each other? Mack doesn't strike me as a womanizer."

Rather than answer me, Shane pulls me into his arms.

Luke squeals with glee as he reaches for me. "Duh," he says with a grin.

"No, I'm da-da," Shane says with a laugh as he reaches for his jeans. "She's ma-ma."

Once Shane is fully dressed, I go up on my tiptoes and kiss him. "Please think about what I said," I tell him. "She's crazy about him, and I think Mack cares about her too. If they have a chance to have what we have, I don't think you should stand in their way."

Shane sighs heavily. "Fine. But if he hurts her, he'll have to deal with me."

* * *

On our way downstairs, I stop at my office to grab a few more diapers for the diaper bag. My office door is closed, so I knock quietly. I don't know if Cooper and Sam are awake yet.

"Come in," Cooper says.

I crack the door open so I can peer inside, and end up grinning when I see two grown men spooning on the sofa. There's hardly enough room for the two of them, but they've managed to cram themselves onto the little space there is. Cooper's in back, with his arm around Sam's waist. He's probably keeping Sam from falling off.

"Sorry," I say, smiling. "I need diapers."

Cooper waves me toward the door that leads to the nursery. "Help yourself."

I hesitate at the nursery door, looking back at the guys. "Did Erin ever make it up here last night?"

Sam shakes his head. "We haven't seen her. I don't know where she ended up sleeping, but it wasn't in here."

I slip into the nursery and grab a few supplies, then slip back out of my office.

Shane's waiting in the hallway with Luke. "All ready?"

I nod, laughing. "Yes. You should see Cooper and Sam trying to cram together on my sofa."

Downstairs, we find Mack on duty at the front doors. Erin is seated in the café with a cup of hot chocolate, a toasted bagel with strawberry cream cheese, and a book.

She glances up and smiles when she sees us approach. "Did you guys sleep well?"

She holds her hands out to Luke, who eagerly accepts her invitation. "I'll hold him," she says. "Go get yourselves some breakfast. We have hot coffee, hot chocolate, bagels, cookies, and a few more sandwiches left."

Shane and I help ourselves to breakfast. Coffee for Shane, and hot chocolate for me. Toasted bagels with cream cheese for the both of us. There's not much else on hand right now. The guys ate most of what was left last night.

Ten minutes later, Sam and Cooper join us, looking like they just rolled out of bed, which they did. Not longer after, Liam and Miguel appear. I think it might have been the aroma of hot coffee that drew them to the café.

While we're eating and talking, Shane's phone chimes with an incoming message.

"It's Joe," he says. "He's trying to see how close he can get to the building."

I take a sip of my hot chocolate. "The first thing I'm going to do when we get home is take a nice hot shower."

"I second that," Sam says as he pours coffee for himself and Cooper. "I think we've had enough excitement to last us for a while."

Mack joins us in the café. "The cops are here to arrest the looters. And Joe Rucker just managed to pull the Suburban up to the front of the building. Your ride home has arrived."

While Shane and Mack discuss getting the outer glass doors replaced, I take Erin aside.

"Come home with us," I tell her. "You can shower and eat at our place, and then come with us this evening to Shane's parents' house for dinner. You can borrow something of mine to wear."

She glances across the café to where Shane and Mack are deep in conversation. "What about Mack?" she says. "Is he invited?"

"I think he and the other security staff are staying here until the outer doors are replaced."

Erin frowns, clearly disappointed.

I reach for her hand. "Please, Erin. Come with us."

She nods. "Okay. Thank you."

Once we're all packed into the Suburban, which is more than big enough to seat all of us, it takes us forty minutes to drive less than five miles home, but we don't mind. The snow plows and tow trucks are working hard, in tandem, to clear all of the streets, but it's a big job.

When we finally arrive in the underground parking garage, Joe pulls up to the private penthouse elevator and we all pile out of the vehicle and into the elevator.

Upstairs, in our apartment, Cooper and Sam disappear to their own suite.

I show Erin to one of the guest suites where she can shower and relax. "Make yourself at home," I tell her. "I'll bring you some outfits to try on."

I nurse Luke in our suite, then put him down for a nap in his own room. Then Shane and I take a long, hot shower together.

"I'm so glad to be home," I say, standing under the hot spray of water.

Shane comes up behind me, wrapping his strong arms around my waist and drawing me back against his firm body. I can feel his erection prodding my bottom. I moan in pleasure when he skims his lips from the ticklish spot beneath my ear, down my throat, to the crook of my neck where it meets my shoulder. "I'm so glad you're home," he says. "I'm never letting you leave my sight again."

I laugh, turning in his arms so I can wrap mine around his waist. "Thank you for trudging through all that snow to join us," I tell him. "I was miserable without you."

"You weren't half as miserable as I was, knowing you and Luke were stranded downtown. I'll always find you, Beth. Always. That, you can count on."

He shuts the water off and hands me a towel, then grabs one for himself, briskly towel-drying his hair. "Come to bed with me."

I smile. "I'd love to."

Epilogue

Beth McIntyre

I t's a Christmas miracle that we even made it to Shane's parents' house in time for dinner. That evening, after we'd all had a chance to shower and rest up, Joe drove us all in the Suburban from the penthouse apartment to the family compound. The Suburban is big enough to seat all of us—the three of us, Sam, Cooper, and Erin.

Fortunately, thanks to the on-site security staff, the street and driveways have already been plowed in the compound, so we have no trouble getting to Shane's parents' new house. The traditional two-story house sits back from the road on an acre of land, right beside Jake and Annie's house. My mom's new bungalow is right across the street from them, and Lia and Jonah's house is located beside hers. It sure is convenient and cozy having so much of our family in one area.

Shane has asked me if I want us to move here, to build a house of our own, but I haven't made a decision yet. I love our current living arrangement. I love the penthouse, and I love the fact that we share it with Sam and Cooper. I don't want that to change. But maybe I'm just being selfish. Maybe Sam and Cooper would prefer to have a place all their own. I guess I need to ask them. Shane said he's fine either way—either staying in the penthouse or moving here into a house. But honestly, once Luke is more mobile, we might have to re-think living downtown.

Joe parks the Suburban at the top of Bridget and Calum's circular drive, and we face the blustering cold temperatures as we trudge up the walk to the front door. Before we can ring the bell, the door swings wide open, and Aiden greets us with a big smile on his face.

"Hi, guys!" Aiden says, stepping back so we can enter. He eagerly waves us inside. "Welcome to the Christmas party!"

Aiden looks adorable in blue jeans and a bright red sweatshirt with a snowman on it. His chocolate brown hair is spiked at the top with gel, and his big brown eyes are glittering with excitement. Tucked beneath his arm is Stevie the Stegosaurus, a bright green stuffed dinosaur with spikey plates on his back.

When Aiden sees the bags of wrapped Christmas gifts that Sam and Cooper are carrying, his eyes widen. "You can put the presents under the tree," he says, racing down the hallway toward the kitchen and great room in the rear of the house. "Follow me!"

We leave our wet shoes and boots at the door and follow Aiden to the heart of the party. The kitchen island is filled with all sorts of goodies—cheeses and crackers, veggies and dips, cookies—and everyone is congregated in this wide open space.

Joe taps my shoulder. "Where should I put this?"

He's carrying a highchair for Luke.

"Hello, Mr. Rucker," Bridget says, as she joins us. She pats Joe's back. "Welcome. I'm so glad you could join us today. You can put the highchair right over there." She points to a spot in the kitchen that is a bit out of the general traffic pattern, where Luke won't get run over too badly.

"Yes, ma'am," Joe says, carrying the highchair to the designated spot.

"Beth, sweetheart!"

I turn to see my mom heading our way. She looks stunning in an ice blue dress, which coordinates beautifully with her pale blonde hair and blue eyes.

"Hi, Mom," I say, giving her a tight squeeze.

Luke is smashed between us, but he doesn't seem to mind. He's far more interested in tugging on the string of creamy pearls around my mother's neck.

"Hello, my darling boy," Mom says, taking Luke into her arms. She brushes her nose against his, then gives it a kiss. "How's my sweet baby?"

"He's doing great," I say, reaching out to pat his back. "In spite of all the excitement yesterday and today. He was a real trouper."

Joe returns to my side, carrying the diaper bag slung over his shoulder. "Where would you like me to put this?" he says to me, but his gaze keeps flitting to my mother.

"Oh, you two haven't met yet, have you?" I say, as I take the diaper bag from Joe. "I'm so sorry. Where are my manners? Mom, this is Joe Rucker, my driver. Joe, this is my mother, Ingrid Jamison."

My mom's cheeks turn a lovely shade of pink as she meets Joe's very direct gaze.

"It's a pleasure to meet you, Ingrid," Joe says, offering his hand to her. "Ingrid? That's Swedish, right?"

"Yes," she says, slipping her free hand in his. "My parents, both mathematics professors, emigrated to the US when I was an infant."

Joe cups her slender hand between his, gazing into my mother's eyes. My mom's practically staring at Joe, and she hardly notices when I take Luke from her.

My mom is tall, so they're practically standing eye-to-eye as they stare at each other. They make a striking pair, my mother's pale loveliness next to Joe's warm brown complexion.

"I'm so glad to meet you," Mom says to Joe. "Beth tells me what a help you are. Can I get you something to drink? Hot chocolate, or a beer, or something? There's egg nog."

I've never seen my mother so rattled before. If I didn't know better, I'd think she was nervous.

Joe smiles at her. "Hot chocolate sounds wonderful, thank you. I don't drink."

She returns his smile, looking flustered. "I'll go get you something."

My mom races away as fast as she can without seeming outright rude. I study Joe's expression as he follows her progress across the room to the kitchen counter where pots of hot water for tea, coffee, and hot chocolate have been set up.

Luke leans toward Joe and grabs hold of his knit sweater.

"Mum-mum-mum."

Absently, Joe draws Luke into his arms, bouncing him as his gaze remains locked on my mother.

"She's a beautiful woman, isn't she?" I say quietly.

Joe looks at me, shocked. "I beg your pardon?"

I laugh as I bump my shoulder into his thick bicep. "Oh, come on. Don't try to pretend you can't stop staring at her. I'm not blind, Joe."

He frowns, looking around the room. "Is she here with someone? Does she have—you know. Is there someone?"

Joe knows that my father, a Chicago police officer, was killed in the line of duty when I was an infant. I shake my head. "There's no one. There's never been anyone since my father."

The corners of his lips turn down. "That's heartbreaking."

I nod. "It is. She deserves to be loved. She's amazing."

Bridget McIntyre comes toward us holding a mug of hot chocolate. She hands it to Joe with a smile. "Ingrid asked me to bring this to you."

Joe and I both glance at the spot where we last saw my mother, but she's nowhere to be seen.

Joe nods as he accepts the mug. "Thank you, ma'am."

As Bridget walks away, Joe continues to scan the room for my mother. Finally, he turns to me, looking gutted. "I'm sorry if I did or said anything inappropriate to your mother. I'm afraid I made her uncomfortable. I should go. I'll come back when you're ready to come home."

I clutch his sleeve. "No. Don't go. You didn't do anything wrong."

He shakes his head, looking resigned and determined. "No, this is her family celebration. She should feel comfortable. Right now it looks like she's in hiding."

Joe hands me Luke and pats my back. "Have Shane text me when you guys are ready to head home."

"Joe, no! Please—"

"It's okay, Beth. Don't worry about me. I'm perfectly fine on my own."

I watch as Joe walks out the front door, closing it quietly behind him. My stomach sinks and I have absolutely no idea what just happened.

"Hey, sweetheart." Shane slips his arm around my waist. "Is everything okay?"

"I'm not sure. Joe just left. He said for you to text him when we're ready to leave."

"Where'd he go?"

I shake my head. "There was this weird moment between Joe and my mom, when they first met. Then my mom sort of disappeared." I hand Luke to Shane. "Hold him, please, while I go talk to my mom. If I can find her."

It takes some doing, but I finally find my mom sitting in the library, alone in the dark. She's in an armchair by a front window, staring out at the moonlit, snowy night.

"Mom?"

Startled, she looks up at me. "Oh, Beth, honey. I didn't hear you come in."

I take a seat in the armchair across from hers, just a few feet away. "Mom, what happened?"

"What do you mean?"

"Why did you disappear on us? You had Bridget bring Joe his hot chocolate, and then you were gone."

Her expression falls, and she look so sorrowful. "I'm sorry."

I move to kneel beside her chair. Her hand is like ice when I cover it with mine. "What happened? What's wrong?"

"That man."

"Who, Joe? What about him?"

She nods. "He—" She stops, swallowing hard.

"He what, Mom?"

"When I looked at him, when he took my hand, I felt something I haven't felt in years." She looks at me with sad, confused eyes. "It was unsettling. He's gone, isn't he? I saw him walk out the front door."

"Yes. He was afraid he'd made you uncomfortable." I squeeze her hand and smile. "He was pretty smitten with you, too."

Mom shakes her head vehemently. "No! Absolutely not. I'm too old to play these kind of games."

"Games? Why do you think he's looking to play games? And you're not too old to want to be with someone."

Something catches Mom's eye out front, and she shoots to her feet. "Your brother's here. I was afraid he wouldn't make it this evening because of the storm. The Chicago police have been swamped. Let's go meet him."

I follow my mom out of the library, and we're at the front door just as Tyler rings the bell. Mom opens the door and welcomes my brother inside, wrapping him tightly in her arms.

"I'm so glad you made it," she says.

Tyler returns her embrace, then steps back to look at her. "Are you okay?"

She laughs. "Of course, I'm fine. Come have something to drink. Dinner will be served shortly."

As Mom heads back to the kitchen, Tyler eyes me askance. All I can do is shrug. "She's okay," I say.

Tyler pulls me into an embrace and kisses the top of my head. "I'm glad you made it safely through the storm. A lot of folks weren't so lucky last night."

My brother works homicide. I hate to think what he might have been faced with in the last twenty-four hours.

* * *

Dinner is a loud and boisterous affair with the entire extended McIntyre family present, including all seven of their adult children, plus spouses, two grandchildren, and some very close friends. Everyone's here—even Hannah, who flew in a few days ago from her wilderness research outpost high up in The Rocky Mountains. Elly and George are here, too, as they're just as much a part of this family as the rest of us.

Bridget and Calum's dining room is big enough to accommodate a table which, with all the extenders added, can seat sixteen people, but we squeeze in a few more chairs and a high chair to make room for everyone.

Aiden is seated between Jake and Annie, practically bouncing in his seat with excitement. "Daddy, can we open presents after dinner?" he asks Jake. "Please?"

"I imagine so," he says, leaning back in his chair. He lays his arm across the back of Aiden's chair and glances over the boy's head at Annie.

Annie is leaning back in her chair, her hands lying on top of her hugely rounded belly. She's only about six months along, but she's already as big as a house.

Jake smiles affectionately at his fiancé. "Do you want to tell them, or should I?"

Annie blushes. "You can tell them."

Everyone turns toward Jake, suddenly all ears.

"Tell us what?" Bridget says, straightening in her chair as her gaze goes from Jake to Annie and back again.

"We have some news," Jake says, as he grins at Annie.

"What?" Bridget says.

Jake reaches over Aiden to cup the back of Annie's head. "We wanted to wait until we were absolutely sure... but..."

"Jacob! What?" his mother says. "Spit it out before you give me a heart attack!"

"We're having twin girls."

"Oh, my God!" Bridget screeches, shooting to her feet, her hands clasped in front of her chest. "Twins? Girls?"

Jake laughs. "That's what I said."

Calum reaches up and pulls his wife back down to her seat. "Sit down, honey, before you fall down."

"I'm going to have two little sisters," Aiden says, raising two fingers proudly in the air.

Annie smiles, tears forming, and Jake leans over Aiden's head to kiss her. Then he lays his hands on her burgeoning abdomen, patting it gently. "Twice the trouble, twice the fun."

Suddenly everyone's talking at the table, sharing in the joyous prospect of two new members joining our rapidly growing family.

Molly and Jamie are quiet, though, and Molly has a wistful smile on her face. Jamie leans close to her, his arm around her shoulders, and he pulls her close and kisses her cheek. Then he whispers something to her, and she whispers back.

Erin's sitting beside me, a bit disappointed that Mack didn't come.

Shane snags my hand, squeezing it, and then brings it to his mouth for a kiss.

Luke sits in his high chair between us, banging on his tray with a toy rattle. "Mum-mum-mum!" he cries, apparently wanting to participate in the festivities. "Mum-mum! Duh!"

Shane smiles at me. "Merry Christmas, sweetheart. I love you."

My throat tightens with emotion. "I love you, too."

"Duh-duh-duh!" Luke says, banging his toy on his tray.

Shane cups the back of Luke's head and leans over to kiss his son's forehead. "And you, too, pal."

* * *

After dinner, we all gather in the great room, seated around a lovely Christmas tree decorated with lights and ornaments. There's a fire blazing in the brick hearth. Liam helps Aiden pass out Christmas presents.

Aiden runs up to me, excited and flustered. "Aunt Beth, can I help Luke open his presents? I'm really good at that."

Luke is seated on the floor in front of me, surrounded by a small mountain of gifts.

"Sure you can," I tell Aiden, grateful for the assistance.

Aiden sits beside Luke and carefully unwraps each gift, handing them to Luke, who squeals with glee every time Aiden tears the wrapping paper. A teddy bear, a stuffed puppy, little cowboy boots, a toy cell phone, baby books.

My mom sits on the sofa beside me, tears in her eyes. "Your father would have been so happy to see this," she says. She leans closer and hugs me.

Shane, seated on my other side, reaches for my hand, linking our fingers together. When I smile at him, he squeezes my hand.

As Christmas carols play quietly in the background, I scan the room. Jake sits with his arm around Annie, his big hand caressing her burgeoning belly. Jamie sits with Molly, holding her hand in his lap. Jonah has Lia perched on his lap, and he plays with her engagement ring as she laughs at something Liam said. Shane's other two sisters, Sophie and Hannah, are deep in conversation about something. Cooper and Sam sit together on another sofa, their hands clasped tightly as they smile at each other. My brother, Tyler, sits alone, watching the festivities with a stoic expression. If I had one Christmas wish, it would be that my brother finds somebody to love. I would give anything to see him happy. To see him smile at someone special, hold someone's hand.

Bridget and Calum McIntyre watch their grandchildren open

gifts, huge smiles on their faces. Of course they're happy. The room is filled with love.

My throat tightens with emotion as I look around the room at these people who have come to mean the world to me. I lean into Shane, and he puts his arm around me.

His lips are in my hair. "Doing okay?" he asks quietly, his warm breath tickling my ear.

I turn to him and nod, tears blurring my vision. "Everything is so perfect."

He smiles, then kisses me gently. "No, *you're* perfect."

Luke looks up at me, smiling as he shakes his new rattle. "Mum-mum-mum!"

The end... for now.

Coming Next!

Stay tuned for more books featuring your favorite McIntyre Security characters! Watch for upcoming books for Tyler Jamison, Sophie McIntyre, Charlie, Killian and Hannah McIntyre, Cameron and Chloe, Liam McIntyre, Ingrid Jamison, and many more!

Erin and Mack's long-awaited book, *Regret*, is coming early 2019!

Please Leave a Review on Amazon

I hope you'll take a moment to leave a review for me on Amazon. Please, please, please? It doesn't have to be long... just a brief comment saying whether you liked the book or not. Reviews are vitally important to authors! I'd be incredibly grateful to you if you'd leave one for me. Goodreads and BookBub are also great places to leave reviews.

Stay in Touch

Follow me on Facebook or subscribe to my newsletter for up-to-date information on the schedule for new releases. You'll find my website at www.aprilwilsonauthor.com.

I'm active daily on Facebook, and I love to interact with my readers. Come talk to me on Facebook by leaving me a message or a comment. Please share my book posts with your friends. I also have a very active reader group on Facebook where I post weekly teasers for new books and run lots of giveaway contests. Just search for **April Wilson Reader Fan Club**. Come join us!

You can also follow me on Amazon, BookBub, Goodreads, and Instagram!

Printed in Poland
by Amazon Fulfillment
Poland Sp. z o.o., Wrocław